TRY THE MORGUE

TRY THE MORGUE

A NOVEL

EVA MARIA STAAL

LIVERIGHT PUBLISHING CORPORATION
A DIVISION OF W. W. NORTON & COMPANY
NEW YORK   LONDON

For information about permission to reproduce selections from
this book, write to Permissions, Liveright Publishing Corporation,
a division of W. W. Norton & Company, Inc.,
500 Fifth Avenue, New York, NY 10110

For information about special discounts for bulk purchases,
please contact W. W. Norton Special Sales
at specialsales@wwnorton.com or 800-233-4830

Manufacturing by Courier Westford
Book design by Daniel Lagin
Production manager: Anna Oler

Library of Congress Cataloging-in-Publication Data

Staal, Eva Maria.
[Probeer het mortuarium. English.]
Try the morgue : a novel / Eva Maria Staal ; translated from
the Dutch by Pim Verhulst.
p. cm.
"Originally published in Dutch as *Probeer het mortuarium*."
ISBN 978-0-87140-334-6 (hardcover)
1. Arms transfers—Fiction. I. Title.
PT5882.29.T35P7613 2012
839.31'37—dc23
                                                    2012025245

Liveright Publishing Corporation
500 Fifth Avenue, New York, N.Y. 10110
www.wwnorton.com

W. W. Norton & Company Ltd.
Castle House, 75/76 Wells Street, London W1T 3QT

1 2 3 4 5 6 7 8 9 0

For Jannie and Suze

TRY THE MORGUE

People make up their own monsters, and then get scared of them.

—*Floris*, Episode 5

PROLOGUE

THEN

My name is Maria. I'm twenty-five. My boss's name is Jimmy—
Jimmy Liu, to be exact. He's a Chinese Canadian. And he's got
money. Loads of money. He lured me away from a company that
manufactures night-vision goggles, offering a better salary and
more "intelligent" work as his assistant. He's broad-shouldered
and ugly, and knows how to convince a person of anything in
sixty seconds flat. But that's not how he made his fortune.

Jimmy Liu is a dealer. A weapons dealer. I mean real weapons: artillery guns, mortar grenades, Stingers, not to mention
M22s, the Chinese Kalashnikovs. Cheaper than the original AK-
47s, and just as reliable. Mud, water, or sand, the M22 keeps firing; 7.62-caliber, semiautomatic, up to fifty rounds per magazine,
with a swing-back folding stock that stores accessories (extra
ammo, pocket comb).

"Here," Jimmy says one day. I have just started working for

him. We're driving along the Trans-Sahara Highway. He hits the brakes, kicking up dust, Algerian dust, dry as ashes. Jimmy gets out, loosens up his tie, flicks his cigarillo into the sand, swings his jacket over his shoulder with his index finger, and waits. I put the M22 around me. We start walking, me bent over from the weight of the gun, until my hair covers my eyes, until my back is soaking wet. We don't stop until our BMW has vanished behind the dunes. Jimmy tells me to kneel in the scorching desert.

"Lift one leg and use your left arm to support the gun." He grabs my shoulders and plants his knee in my back. "It kicks like a mule."

I ask him what I should aim for. The void offers no target.

"Just shoot," he says. I pull the trigger. My pelvis leaps up, my collarbone twists, my eardrums quake, everything undulates and comes into phase. I hang on to the Chinese Kalashnikov, feel Jimmy's knee in my spine, taste sand.

Speechless, I put the gun down. The look on his face is more serious than ever.

Then he says it. In the same calm voice as my father, who used those exact same words when I was sixteen and, for the first time, stayed out all night and didn't get home till dawn.

"Now you know."

NOW

I'm thirty-nine and shopping for a hand vac. It was dark and drizzly when I rode my bike over here so I smooth out the damp *Consumer Reports* on the counter and point at the test results.

"I'm looking for a handheld vacuum cleaner."

The salesman is wearing a shirt with an embroidered light-bulb over the company name. He's not a big talker.

"Basically, the Powerclean 25 is what I need," I tell him, "but apparently it takes sixteen whole hours to recharge.

"Or one of those DustBusters," I ask, "would that do the job? Look, it says here: 355 mm/water suction power, 930 l/min air-flow and 700 ml dust bowl capacity."

The storekeeper shifts his weight to the other leg.

He says, "What do you need it for?"

"Well, we'll be moving soon and my husband is quite the handyman. That drill of his sure makes a lot of dust."

He points at a display case. He drones the particulars, price differences, and extras, like the DustBuster's extendable crev-ice tool, for extra reach.

"Can I have a look at that gray one?"

He shakes his head—it stays in the display case.

I have no choice. I need to do this now, today. Tomorrow is my birthday, and otherwise there won't be a present. I decide to take the gray one.

"I'll have to order it."

"Oh. Sorry. What about that blue one?"

He nods and goes into the back, then reappears with the blue DustBuster. He puts the box down on the counter between us and waits.

I say, "It's a gift."

He says, "We're out of gift wrap."

I hand him my debit card. He reaches under the counter to grab the key pad and slides it in my direction. As I'm entering my PIN, I talk about how convenient it must be to have a Dust-Buster. He tells me I have to reenter the code. I ask for a bag as the receipt comes rattling out.

When he holds the door for me on the way out, I know it's just to lock it right behind me. I'm stuffing the hand vac into my bag when four stores put out the lights at the same time.

The rain has turned into wet snow.

CHAPTER 1

On my first day of work, Jimmy Liu gives me Sun Tzu's *The Art of War*. It's about strategy. Sun Tzu was a warlord, two thousand years ago. The book is way over my head at this stage, full of answers to questions that never even occurred to me.

At the time I start working for Jimmy, I've been with Martin for a while. We live together in Utrecht. He designs courthouses and hospitals. Lately, he's been going on about getting married. I'm not sure that's what I want. Martin doesn't care for Jimmy Liu. Too loudmouthed, he says, and too gay.

"That man has never seen a school from the inside, Eva Maria. He sells guns without a second thought. He's putting your life at risk. And making you work too hard."

I don't deny it. But I'm not leaving Jimmy. He sees things in me that I don't see, that no one sees. Not even Martin.

Every week Jimmy's got something new to tell me. About guns. I learn to shoot some of them. About life. He knows all there is to know about China, Africa, Pakistan . . . He shows me the acupressure points on my upper arm: "Press here and your thirst will disappear."

I learn how to keep track of money movements and make sense of international supply chains. I learn the names of our buyers, where we sell and don't sell. The ins and outs of embargoes. I give out quotes, respond to tenders. I get to see who buys our weapons. I understand the world better than before.

My head is bursting with information. Martin disapproves: "It's not healthy." Jimmy just smiles: "Well done."

He travels, I tag along. In Karachi a car explodes right under our hotel window. In Harare I catch food poisoning.

I pass my truck-driving test. I learn to read and memorize military maps: air, sea, land. Jimmy helps me practice dead drops and conversations with officials.

All is well. Jimmy is satisfied.

My arguments with Martin over Jimmy turn nasty. Then Martin forces me to choose. He backs me into a corner. So I lash out. What for? For nothing, for a point of view, for Jimmy.

The day before my birthday, the whole thing blows. Martin packs his stuff and leaves; he doesn't want to see me anymore. It's fall. I get sick, stop eating. Jimmy flies over. He places a can of caviar and a bottle of champagne on the kitchen counter. He says, "Who needs anybody anyway?"

Months later we're at an afternoon soccer game in Beijing. It's chilly. We did good business. Amsterdam is waiting. But Jimmy wants to hang around a little longer.

Gansu Tianma is playing against Dalian Shide. Jimmy doesn't care about soccer; he doesn't get it. Cheers when I cheer, swears when I swear. Beijing's Workers Stadium is packed. Sixty thousand Chinese spectators eating nuts and dumplings. At halftime he gets a beer. He asks me to explain the offside rule to him. Why is he trying so hard? He smiles. He casually puts his hands on my shoulders. He whispers in my ear. He smells of peanuts and tobacco. Do I want to have his baby?

I've only ever slept with Jimmy once, not long after Martin left. At first my hips moved awkwardly, but then they loosened up. We even got sweaty. But Maria wasn't there. She was off somewhere wondering why she felt so lonely. Jimmy never mentioned it again. Besides, he prefers boys.

We're going for a walk. Jimmy tells me about Mr. and Mrs. Yang. Four months ago they fled Beijing. Mr. Yang was ordered to go to a reeducation camp, on account of subversive behavior. Even if you make it out of a reeducation camp alive, you'll be dead all the same. Suddenly your best option is a twenty-eight-day boat trip to the Netherlands in a cardboard box.

They had to move fast. The baby couldn't come; she stayed with her grandmother. Granny received visitors for three months straight. Four police officers, every day, screaming, "Where is your son? Where is your daughter-in-law? What did you do to help them?" Granny died. The baby ended up in an orphanage.

One of Jimmy's acquaintances knows which orphanage. Sure, he could tell Jimmy. But he'll need guns first. NDM-86s, the Chinese version of the Dragunov 7.62x54R-caliber. Thirty in total. Jimmy says we have to deliver the guns at midnight in the northwestern part of town, near Zizhuyuan Park. Not too many cops around there. We don't have to go to the orphanage ourselves; a friend of a friend will swap the baby.

Then Jimmy and I can play house. "Daddy and Mommy on vacation in Holland." Tomorrow at six o'clock we leave for Zurich. Then comes Rotterdam Airport.

Jimmy gives me a visa and a couple of fake Chinese passports. And a picture of a slant-eyed baby girl. Her name is Su Sisi Yang. But from now on her last name is Liu. So's mine, by the way: "Eva Maria Staal" is now "Eva Maria Staal Liu."

"There was no other way, Maria."

"As long as I get half of your fortune."

He's not laughing. I'm taken aback. I've never seen Jimmy nervous.

I maneuver the rental van past bikes, cabs, and trucks. In the back there's a crate full of unassembled NDMs next to a pack of diapers and some other baby stuff. I don't know the first thing about babies. Jimmy called his mother this afternoon. She knew where to get everything. No questions asked.

It's eleven-thirty, and the weather is dry. Neon lights and cars with blaring horns everywhere. Jimmy gave me a Glock. A Glock 22C, Safe Action System, .40-caliber, with a good, low grip. He's packing his revolver, an Arminius HW 357 T, double action, .357-caliber Magnum. Effective, no frills.

"In China, when you're ambushed by thirty sniper rifles at once, the best thing to do is blow everything that moves to pieces," he says.

Everyone should have someone like Jimmy. Compared to him, you feel like a saint.

We pass the zoo and make a right. Jimmy tries to find the spot. It's a road behind the park. He tells me to kill the lights.

We wait. Glowing cigarettes, across the street. Four of them. I'm thinking: *No car? Are they planning to lug the crate through the streets?*

Jimmy gets out. They exchange polite bows and smiles. One of them is carrying a sports bag. I climb out of the van and walk over. Jimmy introduces me. The man hands me the bag. He points at the zipper. The zipper opens up to reveal a baby, wrapped up in newspaper, asleep or tranquilized. It's got a lot of hair. Su Sisi is supposed to have a birthmark on her neck and a crooked right pinkie but it's dark, I can't see a thing.

Jimmy leads the four men to the back of the van. The tailgate opens. Everyone climbs aboard. They inspect the NDMs. I'm standing outside the passenger door holding the baby, feeling desperate.

Then I hear a thud, yelling, a scuffle. The tailgate shuts with a bang. I step aside instinctively. The van starts up and takes off screeching. One of the mirrors smacks me onto the asphalt. The bag skids away. I roll over and grab the handles. I'm lying on the ground with the bag pressed tightly against me. Su is still asleep. I can see our van disappear.

In the earsplitting silence I see Jimmy struggle to his feet. He's surrounded by diapers, rompers, bottles, and dented cans of baby food. He curses and swears. Calls himself an amateur and me a cow. What the hell was I thinking, leaving the keys in the ignition!

I crawl up to him, with the bag. I ask him if it's normal for a baby to sleep through all of this. We're sitting in the middle of the road, Jimmy with a loaded gun in his hand. I clutch my sore shoulder. We peer into the bag together, looking for a birthmark and a crooked pinky. Nothing. We do find something else, on close inspection: a little weenie.

Back in Jimmy's hotel room, I exchange our plane tickets for open returns. That buys us time. Where do we even start? Jimmy doesn't know where to reach his acquaintance. He was always the one who was contacted. Maybe someone from the street where Su Sisi's granny lived can help us. And what about the little boy sleeping in our hotel bed? Who does he belong to? What do we do with him?

I call him Dopey. While Jimmy's on the phone, I give him the bottle. Then I take some snapshots, for my desk in Amsterdam. It's one-thirty in the morning. Jimmy says, "I need to sleep now, Maria." I turn away. He's not himself. I won't bug him with questions.

Nine o'clock. Dopey smiling, crying, drinking, or sleeping—the roll in my camera is full. I decide to go to a nearby store and get it developed, with the baby in a sling on my belly. Jimmy won't be joining me. He's got business to take care of.

"Keep that gun at hand, Maria. I gave it to you for a good reason."

"I don't get it. I thought the gun was for us to use if we ran into the cops."

"Just take it," he grunts.

I'm walking in the street. People are pointing at me. A European woman with a Chinese baby on her belly. In this country, babies stay inside. The people gather around us. I return their smiles. When they're done admiring Dopey, I stroll on.

A Chinese man and woman, dressed in Mao outfits, cross the street. They're heading straight for us. They smile. The man's knife cuts the slings of the pouch in one swift movement. The woman catches Dopey and together they run off.

I'm nailed to the ground. Before they reach the corner, I hear Dopey start to cry. By the time I start running, it's too late. The gun doesn't cross my mind for a second.

I can't stop crying. Jimmy orders tea. He says, "The boy's proba bly back at home now. Yesterday that gang used him to get what they wanted, and today they stole him back from us."

Am I supposed to believe that? Jimmy nods. It also happens to people from the West who decide to adopt illegally. They pay thousands of dollars, pick up their baby, and within a week they lose the baby on top of the money.

"You should have told me."

He shrugs. "Maybe. I didn't want to worry you."

Poor Dopey. The roll of film is still in my pocket.

We decide to visit the street where Su Sisi's grandmother used to live.

The rental service makes us pay through the teeth for a new car.

We cover the last stretch on foot, passing through a disgusting market: ducks bound together by the throat, a barrel of frogs creeping around in slime, fish, snakes. Cold piss of fear drips from every basket. The alley we take is a dead end. Nobody recognizes Su Sisi from the picture. Nobody knows who her grandmother was. Or they're too afraid to tell.

Jimmy gets mad. It'd be impossible for him to cut a deal with the police around here, even if he wanted to.

"Goddammit, Maria, the whole world is either scared shitless or just plain evil."

The world always leaves us behind. He says he's had enough.

"We'll try a different approach, Maria. I'm going to Quan Je De tonight."

Quan Je De is a restaurant near Tiananmen Square. Everyone who's anyone in Beijing goes there. There's a "second door" inside, behind a curtain. It's locked. Sometimes, for a select few, it opens. People like Lee Mon, or Shing Kwan, or Wo Sun Yee.

They are Tai Los—Triad bosses—who like to get together after dinner now and then. The topic is usually heroin. Or guns. They've been making eyes at Jimmy for years.

Back home, I tend to forget who Jimmy is. The government leaders and clients he deals with see a different man. To them he's a strategist. A master. A modern-day Sun Tzu. A man who's capable of a lot more than just selling guns. Inconspicuous, modest. Just before the camera flashes, he steps out of the picture. Tonight he'll go through that door. Their door. At first the bosses will be glad to see him. But he won't be there to give. He needs something. He must have known that it would all come down to this eventually. That's why he kept so quiet.

It's ten o'clock, dark. Our hotel lounge is nice and quiet. He taps the box of cigarillos in the inside pocket of his blazer.

"Maria, do I look good? Will you wait for me here?"

* * *

I'm reading. Sun Tzu's *The Art of War.*

Make formlessness your goal. Be as mysterious as possible and strive for unfathomability. Then you can decide your opponent's fate.

I try to ignore the clock, I try to taste what's in my glass. And I read.

If you don't want to fight, then observe your opponent; lure him into action and discover his way of thinking.

Jimmy has been gone for two hours. I walk around the lobby, stretching my arms and back.

"If I'm not back by midnight, take the first plane out of here to Zurich," he told me.

He's seven minutes late. Ten by my watch.

Then he comes walking through the revolving door, grinning like he faced a pack of wolves and walked off with their incisors. I smile.

The next day they drop off Su Sisi, a baby so sweet she even cheers up Jimmy. We take a cab to the airport. The plane leaves for Zurich at two-thirty, and Jimmy tells me I'll be catching a connecting flight to Rotterdam without him. He has to take care of something.

"How bad is it?" I should have asked sooner.

He says it's fine. This time. Tells me his market value surprised him. Wo Sun Yee was honored to help him out. *No strings attached.* A little token of his gratitude, that's all they asked.

The weather is sunny. Su is sleeping in a brand-new sling. I lean my head against the window and close my eyes. Maybe I'll run into Martin at the airport. I can already picture his confusion: A Chinese baby?

Of course he'll tell me he's going to Germany, or Switzerland, with some architect to see a stadium. Then I'll say, "Sounds good." Then he'll probaby ask how Jimmy's doing. Me again: "Fine." I'm not planning to help him ask the question that's burning on his lips.

I'll tell him I have to go. Then I'll wish him a pleasant trip, and vice versa. After that, we'll go our separate ways. Maybe he'll turn around for one last look, but I don't have eyes in the back of my head.

I reach the arrival hall. Mr. and Mrs. Yang are waiting. She covers her mouth with her hands. I lift Su Sisi up, high above my head.

REALITY

Someone once told me that moving is nothing more than putting everything in boxes. Cleaning up without even looking, upstairs and downstairs, top to bottom: pick it up and put it in the box. That's why I'm starting from the top, just beneath the snow-covered roof, in the attic.

Two weeks ago—at Christmas—our daughter Nella took Toby for a walk, without wearing a coat, as if it were spring. Martin and I joined her for a while.

"Your hair is turning gray," I said to him.

This morning I could tell the weather had changed, that it

had snowed. Not because I had seen it on a forecast, in a dream, or even on the ground, but I knew it right away. Nella tucked her pajamas into her rubber boots and ran into the yard, followed by the wire-haired dachshund, Toby.

Seems like I can never find the video camera. And when I do, either the tape is full or the batteries are dead, and I'm the first and last one to see the spectacle: Nella making snowballs in my oven gloves (her mittens nowhere to be found, never needed them before); Toby digging up snow with his forepaws and eating it (clumps of it stuck to his jaws and armpits, more and more, freezing harder and harder—later, inside, he'll fall asleep, to wake up in a damp basket that smells even more like him than it always does).

I told Martin to come and have a look, which he did. But not long enough to see how heartwarming it was, because he was blowing on his tea the whole time. After five seconds he walked away, having realized that he needed to scrape his windshield.

I lift the chair onto my desk to reach the topmost bookshelf. The desk is coming with me. I've been doodling on the tabletop for years, right on the wood, whenever I'm on the phone. I don't realize it until I hang up. Slanty eyes, usually. I never notice that I'm doing it. I listen attentively to what the person on the other end is saying. But when the conversation is over, I'm always left with a pair of eyes.

Yesterday Nella and I were leafing through my wedding album. She said it smelled like toys and candy. I knew exactly what she meant. The scent of old developing fluid, or a fragrance carefully concocted by the wedding album factory.

We were looking at the pictures that had me and Martin in them. His jacket was too big and he still had his jawline.

My wedding should have been a wonderful celebration, but the guests left too early, and Martin and I were stuck with all the booze. Nobody understood why we had to get married. Didn't see it coming. They pretended to be happy for us, but kept asking if I still "traveled for work." I tried to reassure them, but couldn't dispel their worries. Even I was worried by the end of the evening.

Nella pointed at guests; I said their names. She didn't know all of them. The sheets between the pictures crumpled up, and she had to keep turning back to smooth them down. She couldn't believe I had long hair back then—just like hers now. Hair down to my backside.

It was a summer wedding. A heat wave followed. Every night I would wake with a start, soaking wet, because my hair had wrapped itself around my neck like a woolen scarf, because I tossed and turned so violently, because I couldn't stand it—having someone this close to me, in summer, in bed.

I told Nella that one day—without saying anything to Martin—I had taken my bike to town, walked into a hairdresser's, and had my hair cut: "So short I couldn't run my fingers through it anymore. Just like a boy's. When I pressed my palm against it, it felt springy. Then Daddy came home. I turned toward him and gave him a nice big smile. He must have been shocked. But right away he said that short-haired women were the most charming and irresistible creatures on the planet!"

I made this last part up. Martin felt that my hair was his property. That I should have talked it over with him, not with a complete stranger wielding a pair of scissors. He grumbled that he gladly would have slept in separate beds or fanned cool air onto my face every hot night. That made me laugh; he's always the first to fall asleep, deeper than a man knocked out cold.

CHAPTER 2

The phone. Jimmy. I'm standing outside my house in Utrecht. It's dinnertime, I'm about to go pick up some pizza.

"I'm in Beijing," Jimmy rattles. I can't get a word in edgewise. "Trouble in Zimbabwe, can you go? Yesterday our container ship from Pakistan arrived in Mozambique. From there, everything was supposed to be sent on to Zimbabwe and then loaded onto two trucks. Fuck! Everything was going fine. All the papers were in order, they didn't open any crates at customs. But now those trucks have disappeared, somewhere south of Harare. Two containers full of goods. Stingers, flares. You have to get down there, *now*. I'm sorry, Maria. Rebecca will meet you there. Philip, Philip Lebesque, he knows all the details. Contact Colonel Dominic Mhlongo and ask him how his son Aristide is doing in college. I wired him the tuition a month ago."

He's playing it cool but I can tell he's worried sick. Two hours later I'm on the plane.

* * *

He's booked a room for me at the Sheraton in Harare. I get there at nine in the morning. Between the Netherlands and Zimbabwe there's only a one-hour time difference. It's cool up here in the highveld.

Because a tribal king once ordered that a wagon drawn by six oxen should always have the space to turn around, the city has broad streets. Among the glass and gold of all the skyscrapers, the hotel barely stands out. Africa smells like roast pig and damp soil.

Last night, in the plane, I slept. It took some effort, but now I'm used to it. I curl up like a mouse. I could sleep on concrete if I had to.

Behind the glass Rebecca is waiting, a billion pigment cells per square inch of skin on her face. She waves with both palms. We hug, it's been a while.

"Here," she says, "the trinkets for the natives." I don't quite know how to respond, but she gives me a friendly grin as she hands me a bag full of American dollars.

"Tell me the plan," I say.

"That's Philip's job, not mine. He'll be at the hotel at eleven."

At ten-thirty I walk into the hotel bar, give the waiter a bill from the bag, and tell him that for the next couple of days he should serve me a ginger ale whenever I order a whiskey soda in front of other people.

This is where I wait for Philip Lebesque, my Zimbabwean associate. He's the one who called Jimmy yesterday about the trucks that didn't show.

Philip and I, we understand each other. There's a game we play with people who try to double-cross Jimmy. I'm the crazy white lady. I shower them with abuse, put the fear of God into them, and then, still foaming at the mouth, I send them packing. After that, it's Philip's turn. He tells them it's okay, he's on their side, apologizes for my bad temper. They pour out their hearts to him, admit to everything. It's a foolproof method.

But I don't hurl abuse at influential people; I have a drink with them. They think my ginger ale is whiskey.

Back in my room I calculate how fast the trucks are moving away from us. On the map I draw a circle around Sakubva Township, one hundred and fifty miles southeast of Harare. That's where the trucks were spotted last. Philip knows the two drivers and their companions. The police aren't doing a thing.

Jimmy calls. We're all scared we may have lost the shipment for good. Sixty million dollars, one half paid up front, the other on delivery in Harare. The exchange is scheduled to take place tomorrow night.

I ask him why we didn't use the freight train from Beira, like we always do.

"The buyer specifically asked for trucks. He didn't want to transfer the containers at Harare Station. Just switch drivers and push on to Kigali with the same documents," Jimmy says. "That's how he wanted it done."

"I'm going to call that guy, Mhlongo," I say. "He can get the police off their asses. We'll see what's left of the goods when we find the trucks."

We don't dare discuss what will happen to the drivers. Tomorrow Philip is taking me to Sakubva.

Jimmy says, "I have a meeting with our buyer tomorrow night, at the Sheraton where you're staying. What the hell am I supposed to say to him?"

* * *

It's four in the afternoon. Dominic Mhlongo is a colonel and chief of police. I have no clue how he and Jimmy know each other. I've never met the man.

So I give him a call. At first I can't even get him to come to the phone. He's instructed his secretary to brush me off. But after a while she's had enough of me, and I end up speaking to him after all.

He says, "I will only talk to Jimmy."

I say that I respect that, but he has to understand the situation. Besides, he's not doing Jimmy any favors by not talking to me. And how is his son Aristide doing in college, by the way? I hear Jimmy just wired over his tuition.

He hesitates, then says, "Aristide is doing fine but he could really use a new car; something more comfortable than his old Mercedes . . ."

"You and I have no need for Jimmy at all," I say. "I have full power of attorney. If you come to the hotel tonight, I'm sure I can solve Aristide's little problem."

He's here. A tall black man with a shiny face, in a uniform a couple of sizes too small. Five whiskeys and a few grand later, we've come to an agreement. The police will comb the area around Sakubva, starting tonight, and Aristide will be driving a convertible, starting tomorrow. The time is eleven p.m.

Philip Lebesque is thirty years old. He and his family live in a chic North Harare neighborhood with running water and electricity.

In the car, on the way to Sakubva, we're both quiet. It's ten in the morning. I can see the tension in his dark face.

"Let's just wait and see," I tell him.

Colonel Mhlongo is a man of his word. The place is crawling with cop cars.

We arrive in Sakubva at twelve-thirty. The township smells awful. Tumbledown shacks, no sewers, no water. Chickens, goats, a mongrel with a limp. We stop the car.

Philip walks ahead of me, questioning the villagers in dialect. (Dutch and English are all I can manage.) Yes, they did see two big trucks pass by. They point toward the city of Mutare.

Women arrive, bearing food. We eat, we have no choice—rice, fruit. We're wasting precious time, but I eat and smile, everybody smiles. This is going to take hours. A girl braids my hair, the chief challenges Philip to a game of chess, minus two rooks and a king, which they replace with two pebbles and a peanut.

Three o'clock. I take pictures, read a little. I watch Philip: he's staring at a far-off cloud of dust—a trail of dust, actually. Two trucks approach, escorted by two police cars. The substitute drivers are leaning out of the windows, waving. We run over to them.

I wait for Philip's translation. Engine trouble. Engine trouble? Broken fuel line, boiling radiator, and no water for miles. Fixed now, though, the cylinder head gasket undamaged. An overheated engine, that's it. That's it?

Philip shakes hands with the drivers, they smile from ear to ear, the policemen are munching away at the fruit. I'd like to be as happy as everyone else is but I'm not paid to be happy. And neither is Philip. I tap him on the shoulder and take him aside.

"They need to be frisked."

He frowns.

I say, "We don't have to do it here. Put the blame on me. But it needs to be done, come on, tell them."

He makes his way over to them, dragging his feet. They're some distance away, and Philip takes his sweet time. What is he going to tell them? Will they even listen? When he points in my direction, their gazes follow. Then they shuffle over to the town elder's hut, the four police officers, the two drivers, and their substitutes. I follow them and the whole town follows me. I stop. They stop. Nobody moves. Everyone's staring at me. Including Philip. I realize it's time for me to take a little stroll.

I slowly turn around. The villagers are sitting in the dust and won't make way. No one says a word. Trying to keep calm, I head for a fallen tree to wait it out with hunched shoulders.

After fifteen minutes, the men reappear. Philip shrugs: nothing.

Shit. Nothing.

Nothing? I consider checking the consignment. But without a weigh bridge? Without a scanner? I know of a weigh station in Harare. But their X-ray machine has been on the fritz for the past six months. Two days is plenty of time to replace any stolen goods with stones. So there's no point in weighing the trucks anyway, here or in Harare.

Nothing? No, it's too good to be true. Why the hell can't Philip see that?

We'll just have to open all the crates, right here, on the spot. Good thing Dominic's police officers are still around to lend us a hand.

"Count the crates and open them," I snap.

"Jesus, what's gotten into you?" Philip yells. Crowbars come out of the police cars. The villagers stand idly by and watch us wrestle with the splintered wooden crates. I want to get out of here as soon as possible.

After four hours of counting we're exhausted. There's blood under our nails, and so far, the crates check out. The only ones we haven't checked yet are in front, about one-quarter of the shipment: eighteen crates of mortar grenades, which are at the bottom, and the huge wooden boxes holding the Stingers.

"Nothing missing. See?" Philip smirks. The drivers are sniggering right along with him. Still, I'm scared of being ripped off, scared the Africans have all been bribed, scared as hell those crates are full of stones. I can feel a headache coming on.

Time for the next problem. We can't reach Jimmy. We can forget about getting the goods to the buyer on time; the trip back to Harare will take at least three hours. We're late as it is and we haven't even gone through everything.

The villagers seem to have dissolved into the night. Philip offers to lead the way to Harare. Without saying a word to him, I get into the car with the policemen.

A few hours later Jimmy and I are standing in a warehouse near the hotel. Jimmy has persuaded the buyer to wait till tomorrow night. It's two in the morning. Everyone has gone to bed. He points at the crates in the trucks.

"How many to go?"

"Eighteen crates of grenades. And the ones with the Stingers," I reply.

"Tomorrow, Maria."

Sleep won't come. I get that way sometimes. Lying awake, I see our victims all over the world. It doesn't bother Jimmy. His grandfather was a swordsmith. He forged scimitars and knives for loving fathers who wanted to protect their families from thieves and murderers.

I asked him how you could possibly tell the difference between a loving father and a killer.

All his grandfather did was make the swords, Jimmy answered. And swords don't take sides. His grandfather believed he was selling freedom. And Jimmy agreed with that, one hundred percent: "We're selling freedom, you and I! Freedom, security, and peace, Maria."

Jimmy thinks it's a dealer's job to preserve the "balance of power" by making sure Customer A is just as heavily armed as Customer B. Maybe he dreams of winning the Nobel Peace Prize. Anyway, I bet he sleeps like a baby.

There are fourteen of us, and we have a mechanical pry bar. In the third crate of Stingers, we hit the jackpot. Jimmy, who never lifts a finger, is standing next to me when they pry off the lid. Nobody was stealing from us after all. Thirty mines have been put with the Stingers in the crate. Cylinders of red, yellow, and blue plastic. They're about eight inches high, and ribbed, like little accordions. They look like toys.

Jimmy walks over to Philip and orders him to round up the drivers for police interrogation. Something tells me they're long gone.

We find similar mines in all the remaining crates: seventy in total. Our cargo was their cover. It's a mystery who put them in.

"Now what?" I ask.

Jimmy runs his hands over his face.

"We go ahead with the deal, as soon as possible."

"Shit, Jimmy, suppose your buyer has a hand in this. Are you just going to let it slip?"

"You and your dumb-ass questions," he says.

Getting rid of seventy land mines. How do we go about that? We don't want to draw attention to ourselves, but we don't want to let strangers handle this either. Jimmy calls Dominic. He'll take care of it.

We head for an open space outside of town. There are soldiers standing by. They detonate the little toys one by one, quickly and efficiently. They give us earplugs and goggles for the shrapnel.

On the way back Jimmy keeps quiet.

All he says is, "Maria, do you plan to have kids someday?"

Luckily, he doesn't expect an answer.

MR. RIGHT

Nella asked to see my wedding dress. She was absolutely certain I had kept it. All mommies did.

But it was rented, so, fortunately, I didn't have to put it on again.

There were many things the pictures didn't show. Jimmy. The people I once worked with, the trips I once took, the goods I once sold.

You can explain all this to a grown-up. But not to a child. Especially not your own. Maybe later. When she's the right age. Ready for stories about Jimmy and his trade. Maybe then I'll be able to explain how I ended up becoming a wife, and a mother.

And why I had to find out if I had it in me to stay home, bake cakes, and read bedtime stories.

I come across some dusty reference books about breast-feeding and azalea cuttings. Our azaleas aren't doing too badly, and I read that book about breast-feeding three times when I was pregnant. I did everything I was supposed to: drink brown beer, eat nuts. But when Nella finally arrived I had no milk. By the third day I was crying out in pain.

Martin flinched when he took the baby from me and saw my cracked nipples. Nella had been making do with my blood through the umbilical cord for nine months. When it was time for something new, I just couldn't get my juices flowing.

Mothers usually can't wait for their babies to be born, but I would have gladly put off Nella's birth. After nine months I still didn't know how to act like a mother, and I feared that my baby would notice. And sure enough, no milk.

My old family doctor even made a house call. The same one who was there when I was born. He asked to see my left nipple, gave it a squeeze. Then he nodded, adjusting his glasses.

"You have nice breasts but you're a lousy mother. If only you were living in the Sahara! If you knew there was no supermarket around, you'd be lactating plenty."

He sent Martin out for Vaseline and baby food. They left me alone with her. I put her down and rolled onto my side to look at her. I thought about Vaseline, cows, and the Sahara. Cows in the Sahara. Algerian dust. And about what Jimmy Liu would have said: "Fuck! In labor for twenty-six hours? I wouldn't even want to do something that felt *good* for twenty-six hours! How bad is it?"

"Thirteen stitches."

He would make a face as though it were his pain. I smiled and thought of the face he'd make if I told him about the grape-sized hemorrhoids, the inflated boobs, and the roll of belly fat I could wipe my nose with—probably for the rest of my life. My little finger brushed against Nella's right eyelid: skin that I had created, made over to my daughter by birth certificate.

As the sky outside turned dark, she fell asleep, with my index finger against her palate.

I realized how strange it was that I'm prepared to risk my life for certain people, when all I know about them is how much trouble they cause me. "Nella," I whisper, "just forget the whole terrible ordeal, which shouldn't have lasted a day longer, or even a second longer, than forty weeks. It's all right, you don't have to make it up to me!"

The chair is sturdy. I'm throwing books faster and faster into the moving box. Not every one lands perfectly; some of the spines break. I can taste the dust. Little bits of binding crumble off. But now I have a DustBuster to take care of that.

CHAPTER 3

I have no idea what's about to hit me. The office looks the same as it does every Monday. No hint of trouble. All our shipments are going smoothly. Weapons are making their way to satisfied customers.

Jimmy saunters into my office, a Havana in his mouth. He brings me coffee. Three dismayed secretaries come trailing after him. He waves them off, laughing, blowing smoke in their faces.

I know what's going on. Jimmy Liu's in love. Again. I ask him if he needs me to call a doctor, but his good humor is unassailable.

He says, "Today our new assistant is starting work."

We've been through this before. It lasted about a month.

I politely ask him what he's talking about. Who he's talking about.

"His name is Victor Smit. He'll be in the room next door. Maria, could you make sure everything's working in there? And make him feel at home."

As soon as he's gone, I fan the blue smoke out of my office.

* * *

One hour later, a boy of barely twenty is complaining about his office, the view, his computer, his furniture, the coffee, and me. His eyes are red, his nose is runny. He's bouncing off the walls like a tennis ball, all coked up. He's wearing an Armani suit, Salvatore Ferragamo shoes, and a crystal tie by Stefano Ricci. All Fifth Avenue, all wrong. Jesus, where did Jimmy pick this guy up, an escort service?

I feel like punching the little punk in the teeth but instead assure him I'll take his complaints to heart and see what I can do. Victor skulks off and doesn't bother me for the rest of the day. I can hear him on the phone, gabbing with all his little friends. Jimmy is nowhere to be found.

Our office is on the top floor of a building facing the casino. The view is breathtaking, as is the rent. Jimmy has four more offices like this, in Hong Kong, Beijing, Karachi, and Harare.

Jimmy and I aren't around much. We work in China, Chechnya, Pakistan, and Africa. That's where our money is. Well, my money and Jimmy's whole life. Mark, the accountant, doesn't know everything about Jimmy's affairs. I don't know everything about Jimmy's affairs. There's a bank in Switzerland. There's a bank in Luxembourg. And there's the China International Trust and Investment Corporation in Beijing. Jimmy's brother is chairman of the board. And his nephew's a major stockholder. Jimmy maintains and controls a separate flow of funds we never ask questions about. Why should we?

Mark and I, we've known Jimmy a long time. And we're only too aware that Victor isn't planning on leaving anytime soon. He's toying with Jimmy. We can tell, even though we never see them together. No signs of intimacy. Yet little bags appear under Jimmy's eyes. Every day he calls in to say he's running late.

"How late exactly?" I can feel my irritation rising.

"Twelvish . . ."

Victor doesn't show up either, thank God.

One day Mark fills me in on last month's expenses. He has a record of transfers from company funds to Jimmy's personal account. I'm shocked by the amounts. There have been some cash withdrawals as well.

Occasionally, Jimmy picks up some pocket money in the plaza and gambles it away across the street. For Jimmy, "pocket money" means at least thirty thousand dollars. By the end of the day I've found out that, since last week, Victor has acquired a Lotus Esprit Turbo SE and a Maserati Biturbo Spyder. Total cost: four hundred grand. Other purchases include an apartment in London, a speedboat in Nice, and a cocktail bar in Thailand. It appears that Jimmy is willing to plunk down seven million for a velvet piece of ass.

Tomorrow I'll talk to him.

"In private," I say.

He sends Victor away.

I choose my words carefully. I don't want him to lose face but can't hide how much I loathe Victor.

At first he doesn't respond. Then he says, "Next week we're flying to Beijing. You, Victor, and me. We'll have a chat with Sung Mah, from Planeco. If all goes well, you'll never have to worry about my expenses again."

He smiles. I say nothing.

* * *

Doing business in China requires some historical awareness. All business activities are controlled by the People's Liberation Army. At one point, the party gave the PLA permission to raise the soldiers' standard of living. This favor created an untamable monster. Within eight years, the senior PLA commanders had taken charge of all trade in weapons, drugs, real estate, and consumer goods, as well as the country's infrastructure and telecommunications.

For several decades, the Chinese government has been trying to get a grip on its generals and officers, but to no avail. In 1993, 40 percent of the PLA's business activities were banned, but the only effect was endemic corruption. From then on the party started looking the other way—the only option that remained.

Planeco is the PLA's outlet store. It sells secondhand Chinese defense material to foreign countries through middlemen. That's a lucrative business. Extremely lucrative. Jimmy is one of those middlemen. Sung Mah, the director of Planeco, has quite a reputation. Ever since a major weapons-smuggling operation in California, he has been America's most wanted foreign criminal. He owes the rest of his fame to cocaine and opium deals.

This week Sung's got ninety T-80 tanks on sale. Jimmy has already agreed to resell them to Colonel Mandua in Pakistan. For some reason he needs exactly ninety T-80s. Sung will probably go through with the deal. That means big bucks for Jimmy. We're talking about a 30-million-dollar commission.

"With that kind of money, I can buy a Monet and have it painted over in a different color," he brags.

I ask him if I really need to come along to Beijing. I can't see why it's helpful for me to go along and, more importantly, I don't feel like it. But Jimmy turns a deaf ear. I'm his lucky charm, he says, and anyway, what am I whining about, didn't I love Beijing? It's true. We're leaving in two days.

At the baggage claim in Beijing, Victor's trunk seems to be missing. "Fucking unbelievable," he says. "The last thing I need is this bullshit."

Jimmy immediately heads for the smoking area.

I tell Victor to keep his mouth shut and then fill out thirty forms for him. I learn about the contents of the trunk: toiletries, a manicure set, two dumbbells weighing ten pounds altogether, a Modesty Blaise comic book, edible underwear (I just keep writing), licorice, an iPod, and a blow-dryer. They don't expect it to show up before next week. By then we'll be gone again. He'll have to do it all over again at Amsterdam Airport.

"Don't you dare take out your frustration on me," I tell him.

In China, you need to empty your head. Don't swim against the current; go with the flow. No problem for Jimmy. He drinks Maotai and reptile blood, eats faster with chopsticks than with a fork, and joins a row of seventeen people defecating into a public gutter—no walls or doors, men and women chatting—without spattering his shoes or fainting from the stench. Together we climb the Wall and eat stir-fried rat, bat, and monkey.

Victor is taken aback by the traffic. It's pointless to look before you cross the street. Just run for it and pray.

Jimmy has made it through two days of negotiations. Sung Mah has shown up to hear his pitch. They speak Putonghua; the gist of the conversations is lost on me. Jimmy explains everything afterward. It's going well. Sung Mah seems interested in Jimmy's proposition. They contact Colonel Mandua in Pakistan, and that seems to go well too.

Tonight we're all having dinner at our hotel. Victor got permission to shop at Long Fu Mall the past two days, but he didn't buy anything because he felt that nothing really suited him. It's the day of the last conversations between Sung and Jimmy.

I take Victor with me to the Summer Palace. It's hot. I take pictures of the sun on the water, a sailboat on the lake.

In the afternoon we walk back to the hotel. My room is on the fifth floor; so is Victor's. Jimmy and Sung are on the first. We meet on the roof terrace for dinner.

Sung is tall and slim and everything else that Jimmy's not. He pulls my chair out for me and starts to make lively conversation in perfect English. The lazy Susan on our table fills up. Sung talks about the food and how it's prepared. I look at Jimmy. He's brooding over something, I can tell, but I can't figure out what. I accept a piece of carp from Sung Mah and smile.

After eleven o'clock and four Maotais, my English gives out on me. I ask Jimmy if he'd mind if I called it a night. I'm excused. Sung gets up to shake my hand.

I know my way around. I don't get lost; I don't get in an accident; I don't get robbed. I bring a book down from my room and start reading in the lounge. Air-conditioning and whiskey. After an hour and three glasses, I'm ready for bed. It's quarter to one.

The elevator is empty. I push the button for the fifth floor. The elevator stops on the first. Victor gets in. Before I open my mouth I can see that something is wrong. Very wrong. He shuffles along the walls of the elevator, shivering, his eyes averted.

I think: *Goddammit, where did that prick get his coke from this time?*

I ask, "Victor, are you okay?" and then he collapses. He's at my feet, and I can see blood on his Armani pants. Now I'm shaking as badly as him. *We have to get out of here*, I think to myself, up to the fifth floor, up to my room. But how do I get him there?

I get down on my knees. "Can you walk? Victor, what's wrong, get up . . ." I tug at his shoulders, breaking into a sweat. Why isn't he responding? Is it the drugs or the injuries?

We arrive at the fifth floor. I help him struggle to his feet. After a lot of fumbling with the key card, I finally manage to get into my room. I leave him standing in the corridor and go into the bathroom to fill the tub. Should we report this? Leave all the bloodstains untouched? The water is running.

Victor just stands there, sobbing.

I start talking about going to the hospital, calling a doctor, warning Jimmy . . .

Then I realize that I haven't got a clue what's going on. Or how bad it is. His pants need to come off. I lead him into the bathroom.

"Don't tell Jimmy, Maria, please."

He's crying like a baby, with long, sustained howls.

"Come on, stop crying. And take off those clothes." I sound almost like a mother. I put his pants and underwear in cold water. He starts to shiver. The water colors pink. Then I start to get an idea of what's going on: it's time for a rectal examination.

Of all the people whose faces I can't even stand, he's the one whose anus I get to inspect. There's blood running down his leg, dripping onto my bathroom floor. I can see some tearing—actually, it looks serious.

I tell him again that we need to get to a hospital.

"I'm not going, Maria!" he sobs.

I hesitate. I can't force him. He steps into the tub.

I mumble that I don't understand why he cheated on Jimmy.

He covers his face with his hands and swears it wasn't his idea. Sung started it and Jimmy said, "Please, Victor, just a blow job . . . you can do that for me, for us."

"Jimmy left us alone. Sung had some coke. I blew him. It took longer than I thought it would. Just before he came, he drew a gun. I had to turn around, on my knees. He yelled at me to open wide, hurry up . . . he pushed the barrel inside . . . I had no time."

Now he's sobbing and howling again.

I don't want to hear any more of this horrifying story.

I help him out of the tub. While he's drying off, I take a few sanitary pads out of my suitcase. At a store in the hotel lobby I buy some inedible men's underwear. Then I stick on one of the pads, also giving Victor some iodine ointment and Tylenol.

I head upstairs to the restaurant and, with a forbidding look in my eyes, ask for a glass of salad oil. Back in the room, I tell Victor to drink it. I promise to buy him laxatives tomorrow. Then I tell him to go back to his own room.

With the remaining sanitary napkins in his hand, he shuffles out into the hallway. I lock the door. Those pants need to be taken to the cleaners tomorrow. *Things to buy: laxatives, more sanitary pads, painkillers.*

* * *

I go to breakfast early. To my astonishment, so does Jimmy. I'm hoping he won't see me but, to my horror, he sits down at my table.

It takes him five minutes to realize I'm not in a chatty mood. He tries a joke: "Look who got up on the wrong side of the bed! Did you have a few too many last night, or is it that time of the month?"

My sense of decorum vanishes. I hear myself say, "You bet it's time, Jimmy. And if you don't mind, I'd better go borrow some sanitary napkins from Victor—if he can spare any, that is. He was bleeding pretty heavily last night. Apparently that can happen when someone shoves a gun up your ass."

As I walk away I realize that I was talking too loud. People are staring.

I'm looking for a pharmacy. A Western one. No dried animals or herbal tea. I buy the things I need, take the pants to the cleaners.

Sung is leaving at eleven o'clock. Until then I have to control myself.

I see uniformed children in the streets. They are marching, singing some song about the Great Helmsman. Their voices fan out across the plaza. I go on listening, even when they're out of sight. Why am I still here?

I turn around and go back to the travel agency I just passed. I'm the only customer. I pull out my credit card and say, "The first flight to Amsterdam, please. Can you pick up my luggage at the Grand Hotel? And have these toiletries delivered there?"

* * *

It gets me suspended for a month. A formality. Jimmy sputters at me from Beijing, over the phone. So thirty million means nothing to me anymore? Was I aware of the fact that Victor had volunteered? Am I planning to go to church every Sunday from now on, to pray for God's mercy on all arms dealers, boy toys, and myself?

I let him fly off the handle.

I decide not to quit if Jimmy doesn't fire me.

He calls me up after only a week. I'm in the middle of painting my walls pink. I let him dangle for two days. He shows up in jeans, holding a paintbrush, straight from London.

He says, "It's not exactly painting over a Monet."

Victor never found out where I dropped off his pants. He's still mad about that, but can't talk to anyone else about it, except maybe to the employees that Jimmy threw in when he bought Victor that bar in Thailand, where he is now.

Sung and Colonel Mandua didn't keep their word, and the T-80 tanks ended up in Pakistan without Jimmy's help. That's why Victor got too expensive to keep around. He kept the Lotus. The Maserati was sold, along with the boat in Nice and the apartment in London.

I'm glad Jimmy dumped him in the end.

HERE

I come across books that I should have gotten rid of a long time ago. Ten past twelve. Nella will be out of school any minute.

Encyclopedias of weapons, old files on wicked men in far-away lands, studies of carbines, mines, and bombs, manuals for handguns and grenade launchers. I should put everything in a box, fill it up with newspaper, take it out to the dump, and burn it.

A better question than Jimmy's, "Maria, do you want to have kids someday?" would have been, "And what were you planning to tell them about yourself?"

Downstairs, Toby barks. Nella's home for lunch.

But she doesn't even ask what I've been up to all morning. She sits at the table talking to a friend she brought with her. They've switched on the kitchen radio. I turn it down.

They are nine years old and could easily cope without their mothers. They'd love to. Unless there's a fever, tears, a bad dream.

Outside, dark clouds, swollen with snow, blot out the light for a while. I switch on the table lamp.

They're talking about a girl who acts stupid. *Stupid.* They're imitating how she walks, stooped over, her teeth sticking out. Her name is Sjanna.

I pull a few slices of bread out of the freezer and ask what they want on their sandwiches. "I'm not sure I like to hear you making fun of that girl," I say. "Who started it, anyway? And what do the other kids in your class do?"

They exchange glances, each waiting to see what the other one will say. I can just picture how it works: one big bully leading the pack, and anyone who dares to be nice gets pushed around worse than the victim. What would I hate most: having a daughter who's a laughingstock, a ruthless tormentor, or a gutless tag-along? Which category do I fall into? What do I tell Nella?

I ask her if it's possible that Sjanna is just a nice, normal kid who doesn't like being picked on. No way, Mom, she's not normal, unless it's normal the way she dresses, the way she cries all the time. She's *stupid*, and have I ever seen her mother?

Have they?

No, well, yes! Once.

I sigh.

They're off to school again.

"Big kiss!" She wraps her arms around my neck, right in front of her friend. Her lips are dry and cracked. I tell her to put some cocoa butter on them, and to be careful on her bike, with all that snow. Yes, Mom. And she's gone.

I do the dishes and try to figure out what to make for dinner.

The movers call to check if I need any extra boxes. I tell them I don't think so. As soon as I hang up, I realize: This is all going too slow. They want to know how many boxes and I don't have a clue because I'm too slow. Half of this stuff should go, but I'm just not getting around to it.

As I'm wiping off the phone with a dishcloth, it rings again. A man with a name and a voice that I don't recognize. He waits. So do I.

"I'm Nella's principal," he says. "I take it you are Nella's mother?"

I grip the receiver firmly with one hand, placing the other on my hip. What is he waiting for? Did something happen? No, it's probably something she did. He's calling to lecture me. Yes, his tone is definitely going in that direction.

My daughter was involved in an incident this morning. The word "incident" makes me think of a news flash about a teenager on the rampage with a firearm.

A group of five kids, including Nella, threw a classmate's scarf into the toilet. And then flushed.

He tells me he's going to get to the bottom of this. The toilet was clogged up for hours. Of course, Nella will have to stay after school until she has personally mopped every single drop of water off the floor. He'll keep me informed and call back soon to make an appointment for a little chat.

I can picture this man on vacation, not too far away from home, wearing Bermuda shorts, getting up before dawn to watch birds. Each time a rare species flies away before he can take its picture, he mutters something like, "Shucks." Back at camp he indignantly tells his wife about the "incident." Every day for two weeks, she has to reassure him that the little birdie is sure to come out again.

I think of how many times I made my daughter share her candy or say thank you for a free ice cream, how many times we read The Ugly Duckling . . . What kind of person would throw someone's scarf into the toilet?

Then I wonder if she touched the inside of the toilet bowl. Doesn't she know that can make her sick? I have to say something. Tell him I appreciate everything he does for the school.

Some days, you wish you could snap your fingers and disappear in a cloud of smoke.

She doesn't tell me why she's late. Probably scared. She's coloring something in with markers, wearing a sweater I bought at a flea market. It was freezing; she had to pee; I didn't have enough money on me; she tossed her allowance at me and ran into a department store. With the sweater in my bag, I found her there, humming straight through the toilet door. Of all the ladies in line, only the lavatory attendant and I were smiling.

I have some remarks. Educationally sound remarks. But I have to look hard for words that will make sense to a nine-year-old.

A month ago she traced all the eyes that I'd drawn on my desktop. Now she's drawing eyes of her own. More lifelike than mine. On the first drawing that she gave me, she wrote, *I learned it from you.*

The wish list for her next birthday now includes a cell phone.

"About this girl Sjanna that you mentioned earlier," I say.

I glance outside. *Reminder to myself: pack the birdhouse.*

CHAPTER 4

This is Kahuta, northern Pakistan. It's winter and so cold that every thought freezes. We are in a laboratory with three thousand ultracentrifuges, which separate uranium 235 from uranium 238. Uranium 235 is needed to make nuclear weapons. The uranium comes from right here in Pakistan. The centrifuge parts may soon be coming from China. We don't ask where the rest comes from; our hosts just smile.

We talk to K., the laboratory director, and four Pakistani professors about ring magnets and floating bearings.

Jimmy and I are tired; we've been away from home for weeks.

After two days of negotiations we come to an agreement: China will deliver five thousand magnets for the centrifuges.

During the final meeting I make a mathematical error. Jimmy chews me out, in front of everyone. The director and the professors lower their heads as I leaf through the files in search of the answer.

* * *

In the morning we drive from Kahuta back to Islamabad. It's cold at this altitude. The road winds through the mountains—light traffic, just one car in front of us. We say nothing. I'm still furious. Jimmy takes up too much space. In my head, at the business table. And now he is maintaining a studied silence.

Finally I snap, "How dare you talk to me like that in front of other people!"

He tells me never again to let my innumeracy become his problem. I can be replaced, he says, especially if I start bitching. That's when I raise my voice: I tell him no one else could handle his enormous ego, that I would rather be in a pigpen than in the same car with him... After a while, he yells, "Fine!" and swerves off the road, leans over me to throw the door open and screams, "Go, go!" All I can think is, *Drop dead.*

Then something catches our attention. The vehicle in front of us has stopped too. There's a man standing next to the hood of our car. He points a gun at us. And shoots.

I come to, cold and nauseous, on a stretcher in a crowded hospital corridor. My left hand stings. It's covered in blood. So's my lap, the crotch of my pants, my blouse—there's blood everywhere. Jesus, do I have a gut wound? Then why doesn't it hurt?

I try moving a little. When I realize it feels fine, I sit upright, then decide to get up and walk. As I stagger off looking for an exit, two nurses grab hold of me. They smell like disinfectant and speak Urdu or Punjabi. I struggle. They call for help and push me into a consulting room.

The doctor introduces himself but I don't catch his name. He tells me I'm in Rawalpindi General Hospital. I have a thousand questions but I can think of only one: Where is Jimmy?

He tells me how they found us, Jimmy's injured head in my lap. I want him to stop. But he goes on, unperturbed. Jimmy is in bad shape: severe head trauma. He was transferred to a private hospital in Islamabad an hour ago. As he gives me the address he says, "You are in shock and need to wash your face. Also, a bullet grazed your hand. You were luckier than your friend."

I think: *Only if my friend makes it.*

It's noon. The sun stabs straight into my skull. The doctor told me to stay in the corridor, but I ran off.

I try to hide the bloodstains with my bag. I need to get out of this bloodied shalwar kameez and into a clean one. A taxi takes me to our hotel in Islamabad, through the murderous traffic of Rawalpindi's twin city. In the room I stuff my clothes into a plastic bag and put on a hotel bathrobe. The pain starts in my little finger and runs down past my wrist. I don't ask myself what happened, why I was unconscious, where the car is, and who found us. All I know is this: Jimmy is dying.

In the hospital I saw my purse and thought: *I have to get out of here.* Nobody stopped me. In the hotel lobby people started whispering when I came in. The manager gave me my key and kept staring at me.

Now I understand why. My face is spattered with blood. Jimmy's blood.

Two o'clock. According to the doctor, they took Jimmy to Shifa International. The girl at the front desk checks, then says, "No, there's nobody here by that name."

My knees go soft.

I repeat his name, slowly and emphatically: Jimmy Liu.

She shakes her head. I tell her that's impossible: the doctor in Rawalpindi assured me he was here.

She asks, "What was the doctor's name?"

I look at her, startled, and stammer that I don't remember. A crowd gathers behind me. The girl directs her gaze to the next person in line as politely as she can. I might as well go.

Then she says, "Miss?"

I turn around.

"Perhaps you should try the morgue."

Jimmy made it very clear to me: "In case of emergency: no police, no embassy. Those centrifuges are much too delicate a matter."

Four o'clock in the afternoon. Should I call his family? No, not just yet.

I call the office in Karachi and manage to get hold of Sayeed Tahir. He is the—fairly young—manager, and I barely know him; we exchange faxes now and then. Who knows whether he can be trusted, but I have no other choice. I need an interpreter.

Sayeed says he'll set off for Islamabad right away. "Maria, we need to hurry. Ramadan starts in three days. Then everything will grind to a halt."

Over the next hour, I clear Jimmy's agenda, keeping all my excuses vague. When I finish the last call and get up, I see spots dancing before my eyes.

The next morning, I have breakfast in my room. One by one, I call the seven morgues on my list. Five of them only have Pakistani corpses. But the last one received an unidentified Asian yesterday. Jimmy's age. Scared sick, I ask my question.

45

"No, miss, no bullet wound."

With a steady hand, I cross the last morgue off the list. I wait for Sayeed. Instead, two officers knock on the door of my hotel room. The hospital reported the shooting. They want me to come down to the office but eventually they sit down on the side of the bed. They ask what Jimmy and I are doing in Pakistan.

The short one says, "You weren't robbed, strangely enough."

They give me Jimmy's travel bag. They glance at the whiskey bottle that I bought at the hotel bar with my liquor permit. As we talk, I fill two clean toothbrush cups and hand them over casually.

"We do business," I say. "My boss owns a company in Karachi."

They say, "A driver found you. He is the one that notified the hospital."

Without any sign of real interest they ask me a few more questions. No, I can't remember anything about the shooter. No, my boss and I have never experienced anything like this before.

They empty their cups and nod at each other. It's still a strange case, but they did their jobs. I ask them about the doctor at Rawalpindi General. The short one knows who it is: "Dr. Mansoor." He's the one who gave them Jimmy's bag.

"By the way, how is your boss?" the tall one wants to know, one foot out the door.

"I'll find out when I see him," I say. The truth, the whole truth, and nothing but the truth.

Sayeed has arrived. He seems loudmouthed and not too bright. So I decide not to tell him what Jimmy and I were doing in Pakistan. But I take him with me when I see Dr. Mansoor.

The doctor is taking time off. Unexpectedly. And nobody in

Rawalpindi General is able or willing to confirm that Jimmy was sent to Shifa. I get very suspicious but try to keep calm. I demand to see the senior medical officer. Finally, they come up with some documents. A form signed by Mansoor states that yesterday morning Jimmy was transported to another hospital: Shifa International. But the names of the two drivers are illegible. My thoughts run riot. Sayeed puts them into words: "What if those ambulance men finished what their boss, the perpetrator, started?"

I give him a moment to reconsider his words.

"Sayeed," I say amiably, "if that's the best you have to offer, then I suggest you get the hell back to Karachi."

He's quiet for the rest of the day.

In the days that follow we are sent from hospital to hospital: from Shifa to Islamabad Hospital, from Capital to the PIMS, and so on.

Days turn into weeks. We run around in circles like hamsters on a wheel. We visit dissecting rooms, morticians, airports. I try diplomacy, angry outbursts, rupees. The search fails, in part due to my unfamiliarity with Pakistani culture and Ramadan, but also because I insist on keeping the embassy out of it. Sayeed has to pray all the time and is weak from hunger during the day. So am I, since I don't want to offend him by eating in front of him. But waiting every day for Iftar, the evening meal after sundown, is more than I can take. The wound on my hand begins to fester, and I come down with a fever.

My visa is about to expire and it can't be extended. Then Sayeed wants to return to his family. We go our separate ways. I have no choice but to return to the Netherlands and apply for a new visa there. That'll take a while.

On my last night in Pakistan I wake up with a start and realize I won't find Jimmy. Dead or alive. I'll never find him.

On my last day in Pakistan I call the Liu family. Joe, one of Jimmy's brothers, wants to come to Pakistan right away.

"I have to go back to the Netherlands first," I tell him, "and wrap up some business. I'll call you as soon as I'm back here."

I unpack my suitcases in Utrecht. In the evening I open Jimmy's travel bag. Passport, bank card, KLM Gold Wing Card. One credit card is missing. His AmEx. I know the number by heart. I check again and again, fingers trembling. I call American Express. They refuse to give me any information.

I fax the manager of the uranium plant in Kahuta. He immediately sends me an invitation for a tour of his facility. Now I don't have to apply for a visa.

But when I try to book a flight to Islamabad, I'm told that everything is backed up because of the holidays. So I call Joe in Canada and ask him to leave in one week, together with his two brothers. We agree to meet up in Pakistan as soon as possible.

Now I have to count the days. From Christmas until New Year's, when I set off so many red fireworks that the neighbors give me the cold shoulder and passersby point at my doorstep the next morning.

I manage to close the deal on the ring magnets by fax and telephone. Jimmy would have been proud of me. Finally, Ramadan is over. I call Joe to let him know I'm on my way.

Jimmy has been missing for five weeks.

* * *

Jimmy, Joe, Anthony, and Robert. There's a picture of the four brothers in a sailboat, taken at Lake Ontario. Jimmy is smiling as he clutches a rain-soaked Irish terrier in his arms. Twenty-five years later, the watercolorist, the bank manager, the stockbroker, and I are looking for the arms dealer. We eat at Wang Fu in Islamabad's Blue Area.

That night I'm alone with Joe. We're leaning on the parapet of the hotel balcony.

I say, "We had a fight."

He turns to face me.

"I wished he would drop dead."

He smiles and says, "A perfect reason for him to stay alive."

Tony, the bank manager, uses his connections to arrange an appointment at the AmEx office on Ali Plaza. It appears that payments were made with the card *after* Jimmy's disappearance. Payments to Rawalpindi General: a total of twenty thousand dollars, spread out over five weeks.

We decide to contact the Canadian Embassy. Harry Banner, the consular official, is polite but reserved. He promises to take it up with the police. We beg him to hurry up, because we think that Jimmy is still somewhere in that hospital. If he's still alive. We don't bring up the ultracentrifuges.

The brothers wait patiently for news from Banner. They are well-brought-up and know how to control their emotions. I don't want to be well-brought-up and control my emotions. I want to know where Jimmy is right now, or I'll head over to that goddamned embassy and smash something.

* * *

The Rawalpindi General is near Murree Road. It's eight o'clock and getting dark. I'm wearing a scarf around my head, just like every other woman around here. I blend in. I roam from urology through cardiology, to orthopedics and psychiatry. I see patients with IVs on beds; I pass by stretchers, nurses, doctors. Whenever someone looks up in surprise as I enter a room or a ward, I smile and quietly back out again.

The Chinese man I'm looking for is probably dead. He had a head wound and a hot temper. He was worthless, except to the people who ambushed him and to me. Hallway after hallway, floor after floor, I search for Jimmy Liu, who once told me that if he lived to be very old, he would prefer a quick death. By a bullet, for instance.

Fluorescent lights are buzzing all over the place, and fans are swishing overhead. I must be getting close to the last room. I look inside, see a bald man with prominent cheekbones, and get ready to move on. Jimmy doesn't have prominent cheekbones. Jimmy's not bald. I stop because the man lifts his hand. Does he need something? I pull the scarf over my mouth and step into the room.

It's Jimmy. Oh God. Oh shit. I turn away in terror. He's so thin, so nearly dead, so not Jimmy. He whispers for water. I don't think he recognizes me, but I don't dare take off the scarf. I bend over him and slowly uncover my face. His eyes grow wide and he starts crying, without sound.

I ask if he can walk; he shakes his head no. A six-inch scar runs across his skull and he's wearing an eye patch. His left eye is gone. He whispers that his clothes have disappeared. I grab a chair and sit next to the bed. I stay with him until he falls asleep. Then I call Joe.

The brothers come down right away. We're not letting Jimmy out of our sight again. We don't know exactly what's going on but we're afraid that he's being drugged. Joe stays with him. Robert, Tony, and I leave for the embassy as soon as day breaks.

Later on I get to read the official report, together with Harry Banner: "Mr. Liu underwent emergency surgery at Shifa on the day of the attack. The fact that his name was not recorded at the hospital is due to negligence, the receptionist is to be held responsible.

"Because of a bed shortage at Shifa, Mr. Liu was transferred to Rawalpindi four days later. There he had a cerebral infarction. At the moment he is being treated for this complication. The doctor who replaced Dr. Mansoor was not notified of the search for Mr. Liu."

It also states, "The credit card was found in Mr. Liu's clothing. According to the hospital there was no other way to meet the costs of the operation than to make illegitimate use of this means."

Banner says, "I knew it existed but I've never actually witnessed it: they drug a foreign patient for as long as it takes to raid his credit card. All they need to do is forge a signature. Then they let him recover, and upon discharge give him a hefty bill for the insurance company back home."

Jimmy recovers in Ontario. The eye patch makes him look like a pirate captain, slender and acute. He says that he knows who is after him. That it won't happen again. That I shouldn't be worried. He isn't.

He musingly asks if I recognized the gun. I shake my head. He looks at me with pity, as if I've failed a test.

"A Chinese type 84, one of those mini-pistols for aircraft security. Synthetic bullets that don't penetrate walls. We were the ones who sold those things to India, don't you remember, Maria? What idiot would try to kill someone with a toy like that? No wonder I'm still alive. What a bunch of losers."

When I leave, he kisses my cheek. He's never done that before.

LIFE AS IT IS

The receptionist at the ophthalmology clinic looks familiar. Where have I seen her before? Never mind, I'm here for Martin. Martin is in pain.

It's Saturday afternoon. We had just started working on our new house, measuring baseboards. Nella is staying over at a friend's house. When I dropped her off, the fog was so thick I couldn't see my hand in front of my face. Martin was going to pick her up later. I still haven't called her friend's mother.

The fluorescent light in here is too strong. Why is this light so strong? When there's something wrong with your eye, the last thing you need is light, right? No clocks, I want to know what time it is, why are there no clocks?

Martin cups his hand over his sunglasses. My sunglasses. I got them out of the glove compartment and handed them to him as I drove. It's his left eye. Tears are running down over his wrist into his sleeve. The right eye is watering too, but not as much. I try to read his watch upside down: ten to two.

We were sent here from the emergency room. The attending doctor on duty had a Disney tattoo on his lower arm: Chip, or was it Dale? I can never tell the difference. Why not both? There was plenty of space. In the meantime, he had finished examining Martin and pushed the lamp aside.

"Why don't you go on over to the outpatient clinic? Shorty, my colleague, will take care of you. He's new, but he knows his stuff. I only handle severe injuries. I'm expecting a perforating trauma any minute. Shard of concrete. The patient probably wishes all he had was a little tear like yours."

He nodded at Martin.

"Shorty will fix you up."

"May I have your punch card, please?"

Now, where have I seen her before? Her voice has a metallic sound through the holes in the glass. Martin and I nod our heads in unison. She stays cool and professional, asking for his date of birth, postal code, and insurance number. She enters everything into the computer. A machine starts rattling behind her. She gets up. Her floral dress has buttons down the back. A floral dress in winter? Not everyone could get away with that. She does. She walks over to the machine. Mid-length hair, too gingery to be called blond.

Perpendicular to the desk there is a waiting area. I turn around. It's quiet. Two men are waiting there, our age or a little older, as well as a mother with a toddler. The child is playing. The men are obviously a couple.

The receptionist comes back with a plastic card. She slips it into a transparent cover and puts it in the tray under her window. Then she slides the tray toward us.

"Please have a seat. Dr. Short will be with you momentarily."

Martin manages to grab hold of the card on his first try. Impressive, given his condition. Without two working eyes, you lose your sense of depth.

Imagine: It's Saturday afternoon, you've just settled down to work on your nice new house. I bought some sausage rolls. We didn't even get to those. Did I close the refrigerator door? Did I put the milk back?

"Aren't you hungry?" I say to Martin. I'm waiting for something, but don't know what exactly. It feels as though I should be saying something else.

The floral dress starts to wheel her chair away from the counter; she's already forgotten about us. I return to the window and ask, "This Dr. Short, has he been working here long?"

She rolls back, looking surprised.

"Dr. Short? Why do you ask?"

"Because the other doctor said, 'Shorty's new, but he knows his stuff.'"

"Dr. Short is an excellent doctor."

"I just thought it was an odd thing to say."

She has no comeback to that. Martin hates it when I do this. The people behind us keep quiet but there's nothing wrong with their ears.

The floral dress hesitates, then says, "Well, the thing is, they're brothers. Sometimes they tease each other. Just for fun."

"Fun?" I repeat.

I know what Martin thinks of me at moments like these. But this time he saves the day, saying with a smile, "These weekend shifts must be murder!"

She nods; at last, someone who understands.

I'm thinking: *"Big Brother" and "Shorty." Clown doctors.*

* * *

I pick up a magazine. The male couple has left and the mother and child are inside. Martin isn't reading. He can't, since even his good eye has welled up. I glance at him discreetly. Now that he no longer has any questions to answer, he's losing his composure. I put the magazine down. Every now and then he takes off my sunglasses to dab away his tears. I can tell by the set of his jaw that he's not okay.

"I'm sure this Dr. Short knows what he's doing."

"I thought so too, until you brought it up," he snarls.

Something else, then. Think. All that comes to mind are things I did wrong. Me bickering about the size of the wall in the kitchen, complaining that the baseboard was too short, thrusting a metal ruler at Martin with the sharp corner much closer to his eye than he expected, and to top it all off, stirring up trouble at the reception desk. (That receptionist still reminds me of somebody, God knows who.)

Someone calls our name. We turn around. The toddler bounds past us, holding his mother's hand, wearing glasses with a patch over one side. A young man in jeans and a white doctor's coat holds the door open for us. I scan his lower arm for a tattoo and there's Dale. Or Chip.

All in all, it could have been worse: a scratched cornea. Eyes wide open, drops, ointment, then some gauze and a bandage. It'll take time to heal.

Martin wants me to stop by the new house to pick up his power tool. I drive straight home. The fog is starting to freeze. People should have eyes in the back of their heads.

"You'd better lie down for a while," I say.

I head upstairs to the bedroom and close the curtains. The daytime sounds are soothing in the dark.

Finally he gets into bed, keeping on his socks and underwear.

"It's really tiring," he says, "seeing with just one eye."

"You should lie flat on your back, totally flat," I say. "Shall I join you?"

Without waiting for an answer, I undress and get into bed. It's Saturday afternoon. Nella is playing at a friend's house. I realize I still haven't called her friend's mother. I'm thinking: *It's my fault. His eye. This. Everything. Every time . . .*

"Very strange," he says, "I can close my good eye but the other one stays open underneath the gauze and ointment. At least, that's what it feels like."

We're lying on our backs. Not a speck of light comes through the curtains. Dark winter afternoon, expensive curtains.

I want to put on a silly voice and ask him, "How many fingers am I holding up?" And if he says the right number, I'll tell him he's a few short.

I tell him I feel stupid. He says it's just how I am: sooner or later, I cost a man his heart, his reason, even his eye. His tone is cheerful. He's so sweet. He doesn't know what his words stir up inside me. So I laugh out loud.

"Yeah, right, I'm a real femme fatale," I say, thinking, *Martin makes a funny joke and I freeze up; I don't know why that still happens.* As long as he doesn't ask questions. Or turn on the light.

My breathing is so quiet that he sits up. I gently push him back down.

"You're tired," I say. "Is everything okay? Does it hurt? How about the bandages?"

He holds me. I hold him. We kiss. He pulls down his underpants—I hear the soft snap of the elastic band—and deftly kicks them off his ankles, then he tugs at me until I'm sitting on top.

"We'd better take it slow," I say. "We probably aren't even supposed do this."

I want to be very, very careful with him, this time.

"So this is what they do every day in countries that have siestas?" I say softly.

"Yes, but with two eyes."

"And nicer weather."

We do our very best. But it doesn't work. I feel how nothing happens, how he slips out of me before anything has happened. I stop moving. He gently rolls me off of him. I whisper that it's okay.

He grumbles at his cock.

"He's had quite a shock too," I explain.

Finally I say something right.

Through my lashes I can see the white blur of the bandage.

It'll come off on Monday.

CHAPTER 5

I'll never forget how to fire a gun. Jimmy trained me from the first day I worked for him and says I was born with perfect aim. A couple of beers doesn't change that. Even half asleep I can still put a bullet straight into the larynx. Or the kneecap.

"Still, you're a worthless shooter," he says. "You wait too long to draw."

That's because I don't shoot very often. Because I'm Dutch.

"Nothing ever happens in Holland," he often says.

It's true: When a person bumps into me, I always think it's probably not his fault. And when someone tugs at my purse, I assume his hand got caught there accidentally.

I lack the suspicion, and hence the speed, to exploit my perfect aim to the fullest.

Our visit to the ministry in The Hague gives Jimmy a headache. I notice that the eye patch tortures him. Three hours of diplomatic conversation is murder. If only he could use his own words it would be over in fifteen minutes. But now he has to talk like a politician. Ministers don't know the words "yes" or "no"—especially not when talking about embargoes and trade delegations.

Once we're outside again, Jimmy wants an aspirin. I tell him I have a better idea, and drive us up to the seaside. He grumbles that he doesn't like sand. And salt is bad for pure new wool. Salt and sand and damp! They'll ruin his good suit, his shoes, his expensive cigars—am I crazy? Without a word, I hand him a windbreaker and a pair of rubber boots from the trunk and push him forward, down the dune to the beach.

It's ice-cold; it's windy; he can't smoke around here. The wind gets under his eye patch.

I say, "Go on, take it off."

He does, and walks on my left, showing me his good side.

We plow on, at first not saying a word. Shells and crab cara-paces crack underneath our soles. Then he starts talking about the trip to Pakistan that I'll be leaving on tomorrow.

It's for his friend. He doesn't need weapons. All I have to do is deliver something. No more than a computer file on a disk. A tool to predict the fragmentation of bullets.

Jimmy tells me to think of it as a mathematical problem. The effectiveness of any shot depends on how the bullet disinte-grates. If it bursts into fragments too early, the chances of a kill are very slim. Jimmy has the prototype of a new kind of bullet.

We're standing at the high-water mark as he proudly shows me a 20-millimeter cartridge with a head consisting of four large fragments, soldered to a layer of titanium. This layer stays intact until the moment of impact: because the bullet doesn't break up until it hits, it builds up enough momentum to pierce a bulletproof vest and then exit the body in four different places. NATO disapproves of this kind of bullet.

"A friend?"

"Yeah, sure," he says impatiently, "a friend. I need you to take him a couple of things for me."

He turns to face me and I see where his left eye used to be. Jimmy has started to hate himself ever since the accident, and it shows in the way he does business. The skin of the crater is taut and pink; a caved-in stump. He has millions but they can't buy him a prosthesis; he's been searching high and low.

Sand blows into the hollow. If he puts his patch back on without cleaning it out, pretty soon it'll start to itch like hell.

The next morning Jimmy gives me a ride to Amsterdam Airport. We run through the details again. His friend is in Islamabad. Jimmy calls him "Patrick" and describes his appearance, since I can't take a picture with me. Tall, fifty-four years old, glasses, a bit of a limp, I can't miss him. I'll be meeting him tomorrow.

"Not at the hotel," Jimmy says, "somewhere in the hills. My friend is . . . popular, let's say. Maria, this is not business as usual. My friend treasures his privacy."

Ever since Jimmy's accident I hate visiting Islamabad, but the Margalla Hills, just north of town, are stunning.

Jimmy hates mountains, except for the summits. Everything between him and the horizon has to go.

I'm traveling without him because today he's flying to Mexico. On real business. He gives me a small book, a Punjabi language course, complete with CD. Instead of exercises, the CD now contains all the information on the special bullet.

"Protect it with your life, Maria," he says with a smile, but I can tell he isn't joking.

He says, "There's a Muslim passport waiting for you at the

airport and something for you to defend yourself with." He means our locker at Islamabad International. And he means the 9-millimeter Sphinx AT 2000 P with a Velcro holster inside that locker. Not exactly standard equipment. More the kind of thing to set a girl's nerves on edge.

The Dynasty Hotel in Islamabad. I lie awake all night. Jimmy said he would have preferred to take care of this one himself. Small comfort.

It's seven in the morning when I leave for Daman-e-Koh, a plateau in the hills. It's still dark. No company but a harsh wind and the loaded gun under my sweater, in a Velcro holster that chafes against my hip. And the disk in my purse.

I'm supposed to meet Patrick at half past nine. I know nothing about him—Jimmy's way of protecting me.

I feel like walking. At the end of Seventh Avenue the hills begin. First, the path leads up to the little zoo at Marghazar. I feel tense, but concentrated.

It takes me well over two hours to reach the mesa and Kashmirwala's restaurant. I'm well acquainted with the view of the Faisal Mosque and the valley. It's quiet.

It's 9:20. An elderly couple is sitting at the outdoor café. In cold weather like this? They speak English. I had hoped it would be empty. Safer that way. The waiter is wiping off a table. I can feel the gun against my skin, the purse with the disk against my side. The waiter approaches; I order coffee. Regular Western coffee. He goes inside. Elderly couple to the left, four tables in between us. The entrance to the restaurant on the right. I gauge all the distances, calculating the quickest escape route.

I can tell that I'm getting too nervous. After all, we're talking about Jimmy's friend here. Is that what's making my hair stand on end? My index finger searches for the trigger. I hear myself swallowing and hate myself for not asking more questions. I have the right to know more about what's going on here.

Someone approaches from the parking lot. He doesn't limp and has no glasses. He's tall but I can't guess his age. Still, that has to be Patrick.

Four tables down, the old man gets up all of a sudden. With his right fist clenched in the pocket of his jacket he walks past my table, heading straight for Patrick.

Goddammit, what's happening here? Can this be right?

This isn't right, I decide. I jump up from my chair and draw the Sphinx.

To my right the waiter appears with a cup of coffee. He recoils. To my left, the old woman stands up. I'm confused: Is this a trap? I point the gun at her partner, who is still heading toward Jimmy's friend with his hand in his pocket, blocking my view.

I shout, "Stop! *Freeze!*" The old lady joins in, screaming at her husband, who ignores us. Then I pull the trigger and fire a bullet right behind his heels. One shot. The gravel spurts up around him. He leaps to one side and loses his balance, falling to his hands and knees. He looks utterly shaken. I peer over the barrel straight into his panic-stricken face. His empty hands are clutching at the gravel. He wasn't carrying a gun.

Patrick stops and calls out to the man on the ground, "Dad!"

Oh God, I was wrong. The elderly couple, the man without glasses, they belong together, always have. They have nothing to do with Jimmy or me.

I lower the Sphinx and try to utter an apology but not a word comes out. Soon the entire Islamabad police force will be after me, and in the meantime all parties are taking their time to see what I look like. I shove the gun back into the holster and start backing away from the outdoor café. Then I run down the hill, into the forest.

Along the way I reassure myself. No hidden agendas, no dead, no injured, no trace. It doesn't help. A disaster. On the other hand: the police are unpredictable around here. That could be an advantage. Maybe they won't even bother to come up the mountain for a shot in the gravel.

To make matters worse, I missed meeting Patrick. Jimmy's going to kill me. To say the least. If the police find me, then they will probably want to know what I need a gun for. What had made me fire. Should I lose it? Where? Maybe it will come in handy after all.

At the foot of the hill I stop to catch my breath. I need to get to my hotel: check out and become invisible for a while. Call Jimmy and see if we can still work something out with Patrick. I'm such a stupid Dutch cow. A headless chicken is smarter than me.

Veiled, under a shalwar kameez and a false name, I book a room that same morning at the Margalla Hotel, next to the Jinnah Sports Complex. Then I call Jimmy.

He explodes, "*Fuck! Fuck! Fuck!* How could you possibly screw this one up?" Once he's blown off steam, he gets down to business. "What are the police doing? Have you hidden the gun and the disk?" He'll get in touch with Patrick but the deal's off, that's for sure.

I want to apologize but he cuts me short. In nine days he'll be in Islamabad. Can't make it any sooner. Then he'll help me get out of the country. He tells me to keep a low profile till then: "You've caused enough trouble for me already." He sounds cold and condescending.

After he hangs up, I start to cry. Once I've calmed down, I realize I didn't apply for a liquor permit, and now it's too late. No booze to console me.

Thanks to the Muslim passport that Jimmy arranged for me, I am able to rent a safe that afternoon at the National Bank of Pakistan, on Melody Market. In go the Sphinx, the ammo clip, and the disk. My fake passport is in the lining of my purse. Otherwise I'll never be able to access the box again.

The Margalla Hotel is not a place to spend the day, but I have no choice. I lie on the bed with a glassy look, thinking about that old man the whole time. Twitching in the gravel, he bleeds to death, his legs reduced to stumps. These images have to stop; I need to get out.

After three days I decide to take my chances. I venture out without a veil and cautiously walk the streets. The policemen all look straight through me. After six days it seems as if I never even fired a shot. Gradually, it all starts to seem less and less serious, less and less stupid. A warning shot, that's what it was. That's all. Nothing happened; no harm done.

It happens on day seven at eleven in the morning. It's sunny but cool. A taxi drops me off at the Faisal Mosque. It's busy. Two officers come out of nowhere and start walking next to me. They want to know my nationality. Then they ask for my purse. They turn away from me, rummage around a bit, and call over a colleague. He conjures up a block of hash.

Jesus, I could have seen that trick coming! For a moment I'm relieved that this has nothing to do with the shooting. Then they tell me I have to come down to the station to discuss how we're going to deal with this. A police station is the last place I want to be. Besides, this is going to cost me and I don't have any money. I pray for help from Jesus and Allah together.

Aapbara Police Station is on Post Office Road. It's a big, empty building. Friday, half past noon. Everybody's off duty, praying. I'm sitting in a room with one metal door. Two constables and their sergeant are playing a round of bully-the-foreigner; apparently it's their favorite pastime when everyone else is away. Where did I get the hash? Do I realize it's a criminal offense?

They turn the purse inside out; one of them runs his hand along the edge. The others get into the act. It's inevitable: they discover my fake passport, they slap it in my face. What is a Muslim passport doing in a Western woman's purse? And why am I carrying two passports? I have no answer. They put their heads together. Their voices turn vicious. I say nothing. They call me names, and when that doesn't help, they shout that I had my chance, that their boss will be here any minute to make me talk.

They blindfold me. They make me sit on an office chair. A strip of light is visible underneath the blindfold. Someone enters the room, closes the door, stands behind me, his buckle tapping against the back of the chair.

This must be the boss. I smell the same aftershave that Martin used to wear. He asks me, do I know what they do with lying Western whores around here?

He has a deep baritone voice and speaks the Queen's English. He repeats his question softly: Do I know what they do with lying Western whores around here?

A radio starts playing loud, screechy belly-dancing music. All of a sudden he sticks his tongue in my ear and shoves two fingers into my mouth that taste like salt and smell of piss and curry. I panic and jerk away to one side. His fingers follow suit but his tongue slips out of my ear.

On the radio two English gentlemen begin a static-ridden conversation.

He grabs my hand and hits me hard on the temple with my own fist. I feel something snap in my arm, but no pain, no pain at all. For a moment nothing happens. The interview babbles on.

I hear a zipper, a metal zipper, oh God, his fly. Then he yanks at my hair. Who can see this? Are there other men here, watching? He turns my chair. Now I hear him take off his belt, I lean away, on the radio the interviewer laughs politely at one of his guest's jokes, he tries to shove his dick into my mouth, it doesn't work because I keep my lips shut, then his hand forces mine to stroke his dick. He leans into me heavily, making my blindfold shift upward.

When he comes I catch a glimpse of his hand, wearing a golden signet ring, and his short, stumpy cock.

I feverishly try to think: Am I still alive? Am I okay?

I'm still alive, so I'm okay.

A police cell in Islamabad is not a good place to get sick. I'm in there with three other women when I get a fit of diarrhea.

They watch me as I mess up their john, squirming with pain. It won't be emptied before nightfall. There's paper but nothing to cover it. The women hold their noses and hiss, making it clear they think that I should ask the guards for a lid to seal off the bucket.

I have a strangely deep sleep, on the floor. I no longer dream of the old man. I dream of Jimmy saving me.

I get an inflammation and yellow pus makes my eyes stick together. I spoon up the runny dal I get for dinner, down to the last bite, gagging.

On the fifth night somebody comes to get me. A female officer puts me under the shower and gives me clean clothes. Then we walk through a corridor. At the end of it there is a door that reads: C. CHAUDARY, INSPECTOR GENERAL OF POLICE, ISLAMABAD. She knocks, gently urges me inside. I wait anxiously.

Behind the desk is one of the most influential men of the district: the IG of Islamabad. He's jotting something down in a notebook. When he lifts up his head and smiles, I notice that he's wearing glasses. He stands up and I notice that he's tall. He walks around the desk and I notice that he limps. Patrick! I want to cry in happiness. Then he starts talking in a friendly way. He tells me that Jimmy's looking for me.

My stomach turns. I recognize his voice right away, his signet ring, and his aftershave. And I can tell that he knows that I know.

He gets behind my chair, just like he did five days ago, and says that Jimmy, his friend, has begged him to track me down.

"And now it all depends on you, Miss Staal, on whether you'll allow me to find you."

If I want my freedom back I'll have to keep my mouth shut.

His friendship with Jimmy is very dear to him, let's not ruin it with crazy talk.

He wants to know if I'm in Pakistan a lot. I say yes. He says that he can go easy on me or give me a hard time. He grabs my shoulders, waiting for an answer.

I promise to keep my mouth shut. I pray that there's an interrogation in store for him. Followed by a blunt and dirty knife, used to castrate him and then to cut his throat.

They give my purse back and neatly drop me off, right in front of Jimmy's hotel.

Jimmy wants to know what happened. I tell him that nothing happened, not a thing. Nothing at all.

He shyly asks me if I want to see a doctor, for a checkup.

I hear him struggle for the words and tell him that I don't need one.

Do I want to eat, drink, sleep, do I want to talk?

"Sleep."

We're leaving the next day. We don't have time to empty the safe-deposit box. Jimmy admits that he should have told me more about the deal. If he had, nothing would have gone wrong, it's all his fault . . . The information will get to Patrick anyhow. I want to scream that I think that's a very bad idea! But he goes on. Did he ever tell me that Patrick once smuggled his parents out of China, risking his own life? A hero, that's what he is, a friend, one of the few people you can still trust.

We pass customs. No problems. We're in the plane, business class, *pâté de foie gras* and Pinot Gris, I taste nothing.

Jimmy says, "I'm not mad at you anymore."

I say, "Nice."

If I want to, I can lean against him, to get some sleep. It's getting dark and it's pleasant flying home, close to Jimmy.

Then I say, "Your friend has a stumpy dick." At first he freezes. Then he wraps his arms around me, ineptly yet gently. I cry. Ruin his jacket. Salt is bad for pure new wool.

CHAPTER 6

Sjanna's mother calls me up. I think I know why. But she doesn't bring it up and I decide to keep my mouth shut for now. Or she's bound to hold it against me later: "So you knew about the bullying? And you didn't tell me about it?"

And then I'll have to explain that we're planning to move and that I haven't got the time or the authority to raise my daughter, for the time being, that I usually do know everything about my daughter. What she's up to, you know. But not right now, because of all the work. Sorry. And that it's not always like this.

She has such a soft, husky voice. It sounds as if she's paler than I am. Redheaded and freckled. Freckled, pallid, I can handle that, no worries.

"I'd like to meet you sometime," she says. It sounds genuine, as if she's convinced that we're in for a jolly good time.

She says, "We've just moved in. We don't know that many people yet. And I was thinking, since our daughters go to school together..."

Silence.

I think about the word "together." There are so many words that make me ponder: now, this is a word that I would like to take some time and think about. For more than two seconds. Longer than the time I have before duty calls on me again. I would gladly lie awake a little longer just to do that. Wish I could.

My eyes look for a clock. The oven clock. Five in the afternoon. In ten minutes Nella and I have to leave.

I don't see a chance to wriggle myself out of having a cup of coffee with this mom. She keeps saying nice things, and in such a way that I believe them. But of course she's just buttering me up. It's a language I understand reasonably well, but fail to speak. I ask if Tuesday morning would be good, for some coffee. That's fine as far as she's concerned.

We hang up.

"Sjanna's mother called," is what I should say in the car.

Some other time.

All the labels and all the seams of her dance clothes are on the outside. This means that they haven't been washed, I never put them away like that. Her tights are caught up in her leotard, clearly taken off together. I straighten them out. Why? Because she would have done it herself if I had asked her to, no buts. Because this is not the time to ask her.

Her ballet shoes. Where are they? I plow through her backpack. I find some stickers, a small purse covered in shockingly bright green fur, and keys. Ballet shoes belong at the bottom. Footwear always goes in first. But they're not here.

I find them, dripping from a pin on the clothesline, under the scullery window, and right now I don't want to know why a pair of brand-new, high-priced ballet shoes, which shouldn't get wet in the first place, are hanging here to dry. I wrap them in a towel, not saying a word, put the bundle on the floor, and stamp out the moisture from the shoes into the cloth. If Nella dances in them like this tonight, wearing them in and stretching them out, they will be ruined. She'll have to buy a new pair with her report card money. Her father will agree with me on that.

For weeks she has been practicing her solo in secret. We sometimes halted at her door, music coming from underneath it at least twenty times a day. We imagined how special it was all going to be. What it would look like. We waited for the sound of a pirouette on linoleum, a forefoot touching down, a gauze skirt rustling, but we heard only violins.

Tonight, full dress rehearsal. She's not hungry. I'm still standing by the clothesline, near the kitchen window. It's dark outside. It just won't stop snowing. I think of a familiar shape that disappeared behind the flakes, after the last time that we spoke, in my sleep.

The sounds from the freeway, miles away from here, invade the house. I think about the piles of snow sitting in front of the porch at our new place. The walk should have been tiled yesterday. But as long as it's freezing, that's impossible. Soon the thaw will set in. And without tiles. We'll be moving in the mud. Mud-shod movers soiling my parquet flooring and my carpets. Marks, stains! How do I cover the floor? Paper gets torn. Cardboard? Dirt gets underneath. Something with cut-open garbage bags? Where do I get the tape for that? Why am I always the one who thinks about these things? I wonder what will happen when I'm not around to keep track of everything. Does a mover come insured?

I run my index finger along a slat of a venetian blind.

"Is Daddy coming too?"

"No."

"And what about tomorrow?"

"Of course he'll be on time tomorrow."

She really has to eat something. An apple.

I feel that the slat is greasy. When did I last clean it? The next occupant is taking over the whole lot. But I don't want to leave things in a mess. I should get some all-purpose cleaner.

I tell her to eat something. An apple? I go over to the fridge. Toby hears me and comes begging. He starts circling around my feet, almost tripping me over. I push him aside and quickly grab for the plant sprayer from the sink cabinet. I aim for his nose without squirting. He crawls back into his basket. I put down the sprayer so that he has a nice clean view of it.

After I've wrapped up a sandwich in some foil—peanut butter and jelly—I empty a storage container full of cold macaroni, more than enough for the both of us, while standing.

"Shouldn't you heat that up?" she asks.

"Bobby pins, under the coatrack." I point, mouth full.

She looks at my jacket. She asks if I'm ready. I think: *Nice jacket. Nothing wrong with it.*

We forget to say 'bye to the dog. He starts whimpering as soon as we close the door. We look at each other, take our usual pity on him. She lifts the lid of the mailbox and shouts, "By-ee!"

We brush the snow off the car.

"Do you know where it is?" she asks when we're inside. She

talks ten times more than usual. She rubs my leg. I start the car, turn on the heater, and wait for a circle to appear on the windshield through which I can peer.

"Mom?"

"Yes?"

"Do you think that I will do okay? Do you think that I'm a pretty dancer?"

My thoughtless answers are all she wants to hear. And I'm the only one she wants to hear them from. I glance aside, surprised at how she's shining! To hide my shame, I shine back at her.

How do you manage this time and again? It's there for the taking, you almost stumble over it. Why do you always need to have it told to your face? Because of a blind spot that you're so careful about?

Five-thirty, no more daylight. We're running late. I back down the driveway. My tires are looking for grip in the fresh snow.

CHAPTER 7

After a meeting we walk back to the car together. When I want to get in, Jimmy stops me. We're standing in the dark on the empty parking lot. He pulls a ripped-open envelope from his inside pocket and shakes a bullet onto the palm of my hand. It's a bullet whose name sounds like soft sweets, but you can use it to put a hole in someone big enough to stick your head through.

We fall silent. The fifth bullet letter in a month. We know that Jimmy has enemies. Of the kind that doesn't send out warnings. But this is just teasing. And it doesn't fit anyone we know.

We're used to having our phones tapped. Nothing new. We've become attuned to it, for every product that we sell Jimmy and I have codes. We use different codes depending on the date—odd or even. Once a week we come up with new codes, we memorize them within the hour. It's a game. We assume that the Intelligence Service is listening in. Usually the IS wins. Sometimes we do. But the Intelligence Service doesn't mail out bullets.

To cheer us up, Jimmy drives to the casino. I play American roulette because it's fast-paced and gets me in a good mood. Then a Chinese girl joins the table with the most gorgeous Asian boy I have ever seen. The boy takes a seat across from me. I can't focus on the game anymore. I start picturing us together, naked and busy. For the sake of convenience I forget about the girl. I'm running out of chips. Jimmy is nowhere in sight. It's time I left but I can't keep my eyes off the boy.

He knows that I'm staring at him. He kindly tells me that he was born for luck. He's Dutch, Amsterdam accent, even. He slides a share of his chips over to me with a smile. The girl nods.

"Yes," she says, "Shen-li always wins."

When I come home that night, Martin is standing in front of my door. Jesus, Martin. He stood there waiting in the dark and was just about to leave because he thought that I was on a trip again. I wasn't on a trip, just late, because Jimmy and I had to discuss a shipment to a group instead of a government. We couldn't work it out. Then Jimmy showed me the bullet letter and afterwards dragged me on to the casino, where I met Shen-li and Jimmy lost so much money that tomorrow he must do his best to sell weapons to everyone who needs them.

"Hi, Eva Maria," says Martin. I haven't seen him in months.

I raise my hackles. Refuse to be happy. I go in first, switch on the lights with my jacket still on. I notice that his eyes are looking for things he left behind and hasn't been able to touch in a while. They're also looking for me, I can feel it when I'm making coffee. In the meantime, a conversation babbles on that I'm hardly following. It touches on everything, except Jimmy and my work. Why the hell did I let him in?

I find my answer later when, burning from the things that we can still put each other through, I fall asleep.

In the morning the phone rings. Martin acts polite in English. He hands me the receiver.

"Well, well, Maria," says Jimmy, "an old friend? Was that a one-nighter?"

I curtly ask him what he wants. He invites me to celebrate Thanksgiving with his family, as well as his birthday. He's turning forty-eight. I can't pass this up.

I hang up and say, "I'm leaving for Canada tonight, with Jimmy."

A shitty test. But Martin doesn't fall for it. Fine, he says, he'll go home now, to give me some time to pack. He says we'll talk when I get back, no fighting. He's done a lot of thinking lately. These are words I no longer dared hope for, although I have heard them before. Once he's gone, I step in front of the mirror and hesitate. Martin wants me back. Is that good? Or bad?

Jimmy Liu's parents live in Scarborough, Toronto. Their house borders Lake Ontario. I come there often. They gave up chopsticks years ago, but at Thanksgiving the turkey is still prepared with five-spices powder.

I hug Joe, Robert, Tony, and their wives, and clap my hands together in surprise upon the sight of their babies. Jimmy's father is an excellent grandpa. Jimmy's mother is in charge of things. The boys become good sons in her presence. Jimmy always wants to leave after the first day. He tells me that he was on the phone with Thailand. With Victor.

"I can't get him out of my head," he says.

Jesus, how weak! Does Jimmy's family know anything about his messing around with that gigolo?

After dinner there is pie. And singing. Jimmy blows out all the candles in one go. His family wants him to make a wish.

When we return to Holland, I run into Shen-li for the second time. He's at the cash register of the tax-free shop at Toronto Airport. Jimmy's buying alcohol and cigarettes, and doesn't see him. I do. Shen-li smiles and walks over to me. He wants to know why I left the casino in such a rush on Friday, refusing to take his chips. I politely tell him that I don't accept gifts from strange gentlemen. He answers that he's not a stranger anymore.

I ask him where his Chinese girlfriend is. Maybe it's his niece or a colleague. I catch myself hoping for it. He says, "In Amsterdam." In a tone as if she's waiting for him there. Jimmy joins us. The boy courteously introduces himself: Shen-li de Vos.

On the plane he switches seats until he's sitting next to me. He's twenty-eight, a biologist and species protection team leader with the World Wide Fund for Nature. He's a spokesperson on news about the trade in endangered species. Jesus, the perfect son-in-law. Across the aisle, Jimmy is trying to sleep.

I ask Shen-li which endangered species he would like to save. "Seahorses."

This catches me off guard. The word "seahorses" has a special meaning to us. Jimmy's wide awake in a flash and I break out in sweat. Shen-li doesn't appear to notice anything and sums up the kind of facts that Jimmy has been mocking ever since I've known him: Every year twenty million seahorses are captured; they are dried and sold in Hong Kong and China at five hundred dollars a pound. Environmentalists want this to be punishable by law, but that will be difficult, since Asians believe that dried seahorses increase their virility.

He wants to know what we do for a living. I tell him we're in the defense material business. Always good for an awkward silence. Most men walk away at this point. But Shen-li stays put. He smiles calmly. I vaguely recall that Martin will be waiting for me at home, to have that talk.

Shen-li gives me his phone number.

Later at Rotterdam International Jimmy summons me: "Check him out, Maria. Two encounters in one week is too much. He reacted to our business as if he knew all about it. By the way, what is a goddamn environmentalist like him doing in the casino?"

I mumble irritatedly that he's being paranoid. He says that five bullet letters in one month would also make me paranoid.

The next day I contact someone who does regular tail-jobs for us. Then I call Martin to tell him that I'll be very busy for a while so our talk will have to wait. He tries to hide his disappointment. I hang up in despair.

Then I call Shen-li. We're going out to dinner. No time for romance. This is professional. By the end of the night I need to know more about him than he knows about me.

Maybe I should have called off my guy. Now I have to watch him put away a steak and an expensive bottle of wine at Jimmy's expense a few tables over. Shen-li is angling for facts about Jimmy but I sidestep everything, at that I'm more adept than him. Then he talks about the Chinese girl, Suze, his twin sister.

"Your sister?" Maybe that sounds a bit too relieved.

The twin sister is a mathematics engineer. She works at the naval base in Amsterdam. Jesus, the perfect daughter-in-law. Then he says, "As head of the Mathematics Department." He's clearly gauging my reaction.

The Intelligence Service scans the air and taps the lines for coded messages. They are translated at the Mathematical Center. Every dealer knows and fears this. What does Shen-li want from me? I really need to get my head straight. My cell phone saves me. It's Jimmy. His mother had a stroke. Tomorrow he's flying to Canada so I'm in charge for now.

I stammer, "Oh God, Jimmy, yes, of course, get over there."

What a rotten evening. My food has gone cold.

Shen-li inquires if everything is all right, and just as I try to nod, one of Martin's nieces walks in. If she sees me here like this, Martin will know tonight that I wasn't alone.

Midnight. Jimmy calls again. He tells me that during her favorite pastime, fishing, his mother suddenly couldn't remember how she was supposed to haul in the fishing rod and that, when she called for Jimmy's father, all that came out of her throat were strange sounds. She was already unconscious when the doctor arrived. The brothers and their father were bickering about the choice of hospital and the doctor had to call everyone into line. Jimmy sighs: "Parents and their offspring should never be in the same family."

Half past midnight. Sleeping is out of the question. I'm sitting on my couch in the dark trying to think. Who are Shen-li and his little sister? Do they pose a threat? It sure is easy to get dumdum bullets at a naval base. Did Shen-li know about Jimmy's illegal import of seahorses? Am I a part of their plan to compromise Jimmy? What is going on?

The phone rings. It's Martin. He knows I never go to bed before two in the morning. He promises that he won't ask where I was tonight. That he trusts me. Do I realize that?

Before, I would have shrugged at a remark like that, but now I'm happy about what he says. I ask him to be patient. He says that I don't need to worry. We hang up.

I stare into the dark. What do you mean when you say that you trust somebody? That you can see that the other isn't lying? Can you even see or feel a thing like that?

Slowly I begin to grasp what it is that's bothering me: Shen-li is starting to resemble someone who is looking for confession rather than information. That's why I can't believe that he wants to harm Jimmy. He can probably be trusted. And the same goes for his sister. Now the final question is: What is Shen-li trying to tell me? Because I no longer believe that our running into each other is the sole result of chance.

The next morning Jimmy calls. He's in a somber mood. His mother has come around but not entirely. She's changed. The doctor says that they'll have to be patient.

Patient? The only family member who knows that word is Joe.

"Her mouth hangs crooked," says Jimmy. "And have you found out anything about that boy, the biologist?"

I hesitantly say that I'm practically sure he's got nothing to do with the bullets. Jimmy asks sharply what body part it was that led me to that conclusion. I'm insulted and keep my mouth shut. He offers his apologies. We need to stay focused.

I contact Shen-li. I want to speak to him and his sister. "It's important," I say.

He reacts resignedly. We agree to meet each other in a quiet bar in Utrecht. That same night.

Just before the meeting our guy calls me up. He acknowledges that Shen-li has been telling the truth about himself.

They're sitting right in front of me. I bluntly ask them why they sought me out. I don't exactly know what I'm prepared for. In any case, not for the answer they give me.

"You probably won't believe this, Maria," says Suze. "But we're absolutely sure. The IS helped us track down Jimmy Liu. He's our father."

I stare at them.

Shen-li explains that their mother is dead. She was with Jimmy only for a short time. She never told him about his fatherhood, but she did tell her children.

"We managed to locate him quite some time ago," says Shen-li, "but we didn't dare approach him. We know that he thinks of you as family. Would you tell him about us?"

I think it over. Jimmy will probably yell that he already has a life. And a family. And enough parasites who are after his money. He'll deny everything. He'll call the twins a pair of frauds. At best he'll demand a DNA test and dispute the results. Then he'll be obnoxious for a month—at least a month. And then he'll sit behind his desk, wallowing in self-pity for everything he has been put through. That is the right time for me to leave behind discreetly a note carrying Shen-li's or Suze's address. There's a chance he'll get in touch. A small chance. You never know anything for sure with Jimmy Liu.

I promise them I'll do my best.

* * *

When is a good time? There is no good time. Even though Jimmy's mother is getting better and business is booming. Ten days pass. Finally he sits in front of me. I tell my story; my eyes are firmly fixed on something just behind him, my voice is calm. When I'm finished, I look him in the eye. No reaction.

Maybe he didn't understand.

He gets up, takes a long filler from the humidor on his desk, runs it under his nose. I don't see his hands tremble, he doesn't turn away from me. I'm ashamed for having expected that he would. He thinks while cutting the tip off his cigar and says:

"I remember their mother. Atie de Vos. Very pretty, for a girl."

"Would you like to meet them?"

He slowly revolves the cigar over the flame of his lighter. He waits for the end to glow. Then he takes three, four short drags.

"They won't understand who I am."

"Their father, Jimmy."

He shakes his head, in the smoke, says he doesn't want to meet them.

I call Ontario. Jimmy's brother Joe is never surprised at anything. Here we have a Chinese who doesn't care about saving face. He tells me to keep working on Jimmy. Wouldn't it be a shame if there wasn't a reunion? Otherwise, he has an idea. Plan B.

"But that's the heavy artillery, Maria. We'll only do that if nothing else works."

A month goes by. I start feeling sorry for the twins.

Martin says, "Don't you get it? Jimmy deals in guns and in dried endangered species and his son is a biologist. Jimmy dodges one weapon embargo after another and his daughter works for the government. What are they going to talk about over Christmas dinner?"

After six weeks I ask Joe about Plan B. Should we even go through with this? If Jimmy really doesn't want to . . .

"But he does," Joe says, determined. "They're his own kids, for God's sake!"

For Plan B I'm supposed to travel with Shen-li to a hotel in Scarborough, Toronto.

First I have a conversation with Jimmy's mother, alone. It's noon, golden light. She's sitting in a chair by the water, fishing. She turns around with difficulty, smiles crooked but cheerful, and beckons me over.

In the evening she calls up Jimmy and asks him to visit her. She wants to talk to him. He leaves Amsterdam suspecting nothing. The following days I wait with the twins in the hotel, for Joe's signal. It's ten in the morning when he calls. We're nerve-wrecked, all three of us.

"I hope he's not mad," says Suze.

Jimmy's mother demands to see her grandchildren. Jimmy's furious but he saves up all his anger for me. I'm the only one who gets to see how mad he is. Toward the twins he is correct and charming, and he invites them over for lunch and dinner. I'm being ignored. Jimmy's mother got what she wanted. She kisses her grandchildren good night. Jimmy's father shakes their hands. Shen-li and Suze are shining, I don't understand what Jimmy's problem is. They nod contentedly when he asks them to stay.

After midnight I find him on the jetty, his hands in his pockets. I offer him his glass, he doesn't move.

"You're making a fool of yourself," I say, "there's nothing to be ashamed of. In a while you'll be glad I did this."

He seizes the glass from my hand and throws it into the lake. He drives me two steps back.

"Do you want to know why I can't do this, not now, not ever?"

He seizes my upper arm and presses me down in his mother's chair. He's had too much to drink. He holds my arm in a steel grip, pulls an envelope from his trouser pocket, and empties it into my lap. Two bullets and a blurry picture of Shen-li and Suze sitting on a sidewalk café. The picture shows two round holes. In the foreheads of the children. The back says: *Parents and their offspring should never be in the same family.*

He says he's going to tell them tomorrow that he can't be their father.

"I would love to believe that this is all just a tasteless joke," he says softly, "but I can't take the risk."

I can't bring out a word. Through the tears in my eyes I stare at the black water beneath me. Somewhere on the bottom of the lake there now lies a glass belonging to the Liu family. I wonder if anybody will miss it tomorrow; if the glasses in this house are counted every now and then.

When I look up, Jimmy has left.

CHAPTER 8

I'm standing outside, in the snow, pressing down a full garbage bag with my foot. We always have more garbage than the neighbors.

I saw this product on TV, a can compressor. It was at night. I couldn't sleep. Again.

The man used the appliance to crush an enormous bag of cans. All you had to do was pull a lever. A disk as flat as a hubcap was all that was left.

It's just that Martin takes such a strong dislike to these programs, otherwise I would have bought one. All those empty cans of Coca-Cola, beer, and dog food take up a lot of space.

Our appointment comes back to mind when I see her close the garden gate. Wet snow is falling on my hands. They are swollen, cold, and red. I've been at it for a while and it's snowing pretty hard.

It seems as if she doesn't progress. Something between drifting and floating. Perhaps it's because of the flakes, they distort everything.

A troublesome conversation asks for preparation. Your lipstick needs to match your sweater and the coffee has to be made in advance. After all, I'm not too good at listening, nodding, answering, and scrambling together a tray, milk, sugar, sweetener, spoons, and biscuits, all at the same time.

I feel meltwater running down my neck, know full well what I look like with wet hair.

She seems younger than I am, hard to judge, pale indeed, to my astonishment, like she used to have more freckles. Looks like? Dreamy goldfish. Little squirrel.

She asks a question. Her voice goes well with her full lashes.

"How's your husband's eye?" she asks.

The receptionist at the clinic! Finally I know why, back then, I thought I'd seen her before: in the schoolyard!

"I've only just noticed myself," she says, smiling.

I reach out my hand.

"Eva Maria."

"Mirjam."

She puts some sweetener in her tea. I drink coffee. Should I get her an ashtray? No, no need, I guess.

"Sorry about the mess," I say, "all these boxes."

She looks around.

"Are you moving very soon?"

"In three weeks."

"Far away?"

"No," I say, "just down the neighborhood. Anyway, it's still a disaster."

I offer her a chocolate chip cookie.

We strike up a trivial conversation. It's not about bullying. Not about Sjanna. It's about moving and ophthalmologists.

I kept asking myself, what kind of loving mother would instantly believe that her child slipped someone else's scarf down a toilet? And then flush? A loving mother would think: *My child doesn't do that.*

What I always think is: *That sounds like something Nella could have done. Or me, when I was her age.* Not that it makes me proud. But I do believe it, can picture it right away. I should start worrying about that too sometime.

"Sjanna and I have been living here for only six months," she says. She doesn't say "we" or "my husband and I." What does that mean? Should I ask her something now? Is she divorced? Did her husband die? Did she always have a kid? Without a man?

She's not wearing a ring. But neither am I. My fingers have thickened over the last few years. It was on too tight. One day I took it off.

We were driving to a dinner party. A month had already passed.

"Where's your ring?" Martin asked. He must have noticed earlier because his eyes were on the road, we were in the dark, and he couldn't have felt it, since both hands were on the wheel.

"It was too tight."

Silence. How did he sound? Indifferent? Disappointed? He didn't have to worry about it, I could explain.

"Do you mind?" I asked.

"Yes, I would think so, yes."

"Oh . . . But it really hurt."

"You could have had it widened. They just melt some gold in between."

"But then it wouldn't be my ring anymore, would it? They would have to saw it in half first. And then it won't be my ring anymore."

"Nonsense. Have you talked to the jeweler yet?"

I shook my head.

Why couldn't I explain? That sawing in half and soldering would be much worse than not wearing?

She says, "My husband works abroad. He flies over once a month."

Is that enough, once a month? I wouldn't know. A fight once a month, sex once a month. But not too intense, it just makes leaving again more complicated. A father for your child once a month.

She looks caring. I thought the same when I saw her behind the desk. The type that would pull over when you're hitching a ride in the rain. Even though she knows that your daughter is bullying hers. Yes, she would pull over, no matter what. And Sjanna would do the same, probably. That's why they push her around. What does that say about me? I never got bullied. Neither did Nella.

"What does your husband do for a living?" I ask.

What I want to ask is: "Shouldn't we be talking about something else now? Nella will be back from school soon and by that time I want you out of here."

I notice her hands. The many veins, the skinny phalanges. The hands of a girl.

"He runs a business in Hong Kong."

A place that's never mentioned in this house. Not that it's forbidden, I just can't think of one single homely situation or conversation that shouldn't lack the words "Hong Kong."

I slant my head. I try to pick up the thread but it's as if I no longer master the naturalness of conversation.

"A business in Hong Kong," I repeat.

"Yes. But what I wanted to talk to you about . . ."

Behind her a little moth is fluttering, or is it a butterfly, against the windowpane. I look at Mirjam. She's about to tell me something much worse than the incident with the scarf and the toilet. And I don't have a line.

"We don't know that many people around here. Would your Nella like to come over sometime and play with Sjanna?"

I think she's serious.

I look over her shoulder at the little moth. She turns her head around. But there's nothing to see anymore.

"So, what do you want?" I ask Nella. "You name it. Play over there, play over here; just the two of you, or do we take her out to the fair?"

"You should have told me."

"Her mother called me out of the blue. You're the one who started bullying her. And much longer ago than you told me. You can almost call that lying."

Look who's talking, I think.

She sits upright across from me in the hall, on top of two full boxes, legs extended, hands crossed, between her knees. There's a red smudge on her sleeve. Paint? Marker? Nail polish? The boxes smell like dog food, as if they once carried boxes of dog chow.

All of a sudden I think of a raincoat, Givenchy, in the left box. A present from Jimmy. I would like to try it on again. In front of a mirror in different light. Or is it the right box? Of course, you'll never get the smell of dog food out again. The dry cleaner's, maybe? As long as it's in the box I can pretend it's still my size.

She asks why she can't decide who she wants to play with on her own.

"Simple, Nella: me grown-up, you kid. You bully, I have to deal with it. So, take her to the fair, then?"

I get up and leave her behind. With every step toward the kitchen counter I sense her despair growing. I'm not going to say that I understand.

CHAPTER 9

We have to move fast, real fast. As soon as the chopper lands, two soldiers come running to us. They take our shoes away, throw us some helmets. I miss mine and graze my knuckles. While the rotator keeps spinning above our heads, we have to put on Russian uniforms over our clothes in the rain. Welcome to Ingushetia, neighboring country of Chechnya.

Jimmy's army boots won't lace up past his instep. He curses: "Dammit, these things are way too small!"

Mine are too big. We swap but they still don't fit. The soldiers beckon with pressed lips, they want to leave. I ask, "Who are these guys?"

Jimmy isn't interested: "Who cares? Sorry-type-of-Russians."

We know nothing about them, except that they look under-fed, tired, and tense, and that they have been bribed by V., a Chechen who wants to talk to us. As soon as we have cleared the helicopter they introduce themselves curtly: Pavel, Aleksei. Do we know how to handle a Kalashnikov? We nod. They shove us into a jeep, machine gun and all. The bombed oil wells around us—130 of them—are spewing soot. When I blow my nose, black snot comes out. Jimmy has a bad cough.

Along the way the drizzle changes into a downpour. The two-lane road from Ingushetia to Grozny has been under heavy fire and, together with Pavel, we have to get out all the time to help navigate the car around mud pools left by grenade impacts. After a few miles we're drenched and filthy. Pavel and Aleksei don't talk to us. We shouldn't be here and they can't help us.

It's afternoon time. "Nervous?" I ask Jimmy, he's been a little absentminded these past days.

The jeep approaches the first Russian checkpoint.

Pre-1995 Grozny is the best-kept secret of the North Caucasus region. I can remember parks and squares, the footbridge over the Sunzha River. The flower beds on the banks; hardly anybody knows how beautiful it was. I've never returned there after the Russians decided to once again "liberate" Chechnya hard-handedly, starting from the end of 1999 until early 2000.

I prepare myself for the worst. I know the facts by heart. Chechnya has an area of 6,000 square miles and a population of 1.2 million. Ever since the beginning of the most recent war with the Russian Federation, 260,000 Chechens have been uprooted and on the run. About 72 percent have survived mortar fire and 60 percent have witnessed their child, partner, or parents being arrested, tortured, raped, or killed right in front of their eyes. Of the Chechens that managed to escape, 45 percent have seen their houses go up in flames more than twice.

Jimmy and I are on our way to a confederate that never wanted to be one, for centuries back. It's always the same thing:

in peacetime the clan leaders are after each other's blood, whenever there's an outside threat they form an alliance to wipe out the intruders. And still the story goes that for every Chechen ten Russians have to be deployed. This second war has cost the lives of 25,000 Chechen civilians so far. You can add those to the 80,000 casualties from the first war, between 1995 and 1996.

The man we are visiting formed a modest underground army to liberate Chechnya some twenty years ago. Now he's the godfather of a crime organization. At first I hesitated to do business with this V.

"Act your age, Maria," Jimmy sneered. "Everyone who's gone bad was good at first. Besides, when you've held a sledgehammer half your life, the whole world starts to look like a nail."

We notice immediately that the Russian soldiers at the checkpoint know who we are. No identification needed, we can drive on. It seems that V.'s power also reaches into enemy territory.

I look at Jimmy. Ever since he lost an eye he likes to bug the world, especially me. Still, he didn't complain, just now, in the rain, except for the boots, that is. Yesterday evening he was winning big time in a Taiwan casino, ten lover boys at every finger, he couldn't even bother to pick up a stray chip. Today he's crawling through the mud on his knees. I think of the conversation that I had with Mark the accountant: "Jimmy is, once again, spending money on Victor faster than he earns it, Maria. I really hope that some big business is coming up."

It has stopped raining. For the first time I look outside attentively. It will be a while before it gets dark. We're driving through the steppe, miles of moonscape covered in grass. No trees, few pastures, no flowers, no animals, no people. I don't know if it's because of the war. I've been to Grozny twice, always from the northeast, through Sheykh Mansur Airport, but that became a military base in '99. It was the first strategic target to be bombed by the Russians from the air. Then the oil refinery and the telephone central office followed. After that, a group of six thousand Chechen rebels and mercenaries rallied in the mountains.

Three plotlines tell the story of this area. The battle between radical Muslims and nonradical Muslims, the inequality between a corrupt elite and regular citizens, and the war between the Russian Federation and Chechnya. These three plotlines got entangled and now form a gruesome drama against the background of the thirty million dollars that Osama bin Laden donated to the Chechen resistance, an oil supply of five hundred thousand tons right under Grozny, and countless kidnappings of Western journalists and humanitarians by gangsters and Muslim extremists who call themselves resistance fighters.

Not that many Europeans are interested in what happens here. The discovery of a bag containing the heads of four Western engineers on the side of the road to Urus-Martan, on December 8, 1998, didn't even make it into most of the papers in the West. Neither did the pamphlet that the Russian air force disseminated over Grozny on December 5, 1999. It was a message to the citizens: *Whoever stays in the city will be considered a terrorist or a gangster and will be killed.*

Four days later the ultimatum ran out. The Russians destroyed the city until there was nothing left to defend. The Russian government claimed that there were "no more than fifteen thousand civilians" in the city at that time. According to a group of Chechen exiles, there were more than fifty thousand.

* * *

Suddenly I spot a tree. In fact it's no longer a tree. A scorched stake sieved with bullet holes is all that is left of it. The surrounding grass is burned. I prod Jimmy. In between two shelled farm buildings stands a horse in a bomb crater. A skinny white horse in the middle of a swamp. As we pass it I think: *How long has this animal been tied up? It has nothing to eat and can't get out. Where's the owner?*

Jimmy calls out, "Stop!"

He taps Aleksei on the shoulder. Aleksei brakes, astonished.

"Come, Maria," Jimmy says.

He puts the Kalashnikov in the backseat and helps me get out of the car. The soldiers stare at us. Jimmy gestures that we want to stretch our legs. Aleksei looks at his watch. Pavel starts talking to him in an excited way.

"Come," Jimmy says again.

He struts into the charred pasture. Pavel screams at us. Probably something like, "Stay here, motherfuckers!"

Helicopters come and go. The noise drones in my skull and gives me a headache.

When I look back I see that the soldiers have replaced their haste with fatalism and lit up cigarettes.

The horse is up to its shins in muck. When Jimmy has managed to slither down, he first strokes the head. Slowly he starts caressing the neck. The horse rests its nose against his chest, the wet mane drapes across Jimmy's fingers. We're so grimy that it all doesn't matter anymore.

"Here, take over," he says, "it needs to eat, I'll get something."

Before I can say a word he's scrambling in the direction of the ruins. I approach the animal and shiver. What do you say to a horse under these circumstances? Another helicopter rattles by. I slip to the side a little. We've petted the front of the animal but haven't looked at its hind yet. There's something wrong with it. The horse is standing on only three legs. When I carefully wade a little farther I discover that a quarter of the right hind leg has been shot off. The stump isn't bloody but black; the churning maggots make me shrink back.

I see Jimmy walking out of the bombed house. I want to shout that the horse is in pain but suddenly notice how he presses a handkerchief against his mouth. Oh God. He's vomiting. I clamber up, then run to him. The soldiers are alarmed and walk into the field. Jimmy stammers, "Jesus Christ. Dead children. Jesus Christ, shit. Barely six years old, Maria. Three children and a woman. Don't go in, Maria. Not you."

I have to say something about the horse, something positive, something that sounds as if there is a choice: "The horse," I say shivering, "it's missing a hoof, a leg. But maybe it's not that bad, maybe we can find someone in Grozny who can pick it up and take it to the vet."

We sag down on a piece of rubble and see how, twenty yards away, Aleksei is looking at his watch again. He stamps out his butt, jumps into the pit, puts the barrel of his AK-47 to the horse's neck, and pulls the trigger. The horse's head tilts back and its body keels over. We see the carrion drop. Pavel jumps aside just in time. His angry scream is a round black hole in his face, drowned out by the sound of helicopters thundering by endlessly.

In the backseat I start preaching to Jimmy, trembling. About his extravagance and about Victor. I'm craving an argument. I'm begging for a fight, for God's sake, pull me back into it.

I tease despondently, "And poor Mark trying to turn red numbers into black ones. You will have to earn back every cent that you and your little friend made disappear right here, in this fun park. Otherwise the ship will sink, Jimmy! Think you can do that? Or do you see something nice around here that you really want to buy?"

But Jimmy doesn't reply. He just coughs. I think he regrets this trip, perhaps even other things. The bullet letters have stopped, apparently, since he got in touch with Shen-li and Suze again. Not that he told me anything about that. I heard it from Shen-li.

Jimmy and I: we talk so little.

Then we drive into town and from that moment on there's nothing left to do but *be* here. We can't escape the stench of the destroyed sewer drain that spilled its contents onto the streets. Not a single pipe is left intact, there's no more running water. For weeks now, I imagine, everyone has been relieving themselves outside, crouched amid debris.

"Minutka Square." Pavel points, but all I see are a hole and a pile of stones. Every building that stood here has been pulverized. What happened to Lenina Street, exiting onto this square? I look for a point of reference but can't make out east, west, north, or south. Everything's gone, the entire city is a heap of scorched stones.

I'm hit by a wave of panic, I gasp for air. This is impossible! I want to stand up in the jeep, Jimmy's elbow holds me back. My God, Rotterdam was Disneyland compared to this.

"Where is everything?" I scream above the noise of the engine and the helicopter blades; I feel that I'm about to faint. Pavel pulls the jeep on the side of God knows which road.

"Where are we?" I scream in Jimmy's face. "What *is* this? *This! Ask!*"

Jimmy tries to restrain me with all his strength. The soldiers turn around, bewildered. Jimmy screams at them, smiling, "She's never been to a war zone before."

He firmly pulls me down next to him and hisses, "Goddammit, do you want to get us killed? *Get a grip on yourself!*"

I press my fists against my mouth to breathe less. The city center of Grozny is gone. The presidential palace gone, the circus, the office buildings, the university, we're looking out on a parking lot the size of a military cemetery. For the first time in all the years I've been working for Jimmy, superstition hits me like a kick in the gut: this is the spot where the ghosts of dead arms dealers have to roam around eternally.

Is there no electricity at all or is there a curfew? The night is so black that my head swims; my inner ear can't tell the difference anymore between down and up.

Aleksei switches on the fog lamps of the jeep in a flash and targets a wall made up of ferroconcrete and glass shards. He stops the car, the motor keeps running. We grope our way out, AK-47 pressed tight to the chest. Jimmy asks what's keeping me. We have to strip off the uniforms, put our shoes back on.

Then a pair of headlights ignites about twenty yards away. They shine onto a Mercedes with three men coming out of it. One of them is wearing specs. That's V. I recognize him from an earlier encounter in England. Jimmy whispers something. Only the man gets through to me.

Aleksei relieves us of our Kalashnikovs. He and Pavel stay behind, while we walk over to V. and his royal household, since he's already walking in our direction. Come halfway, V. shakes Jimmy's hand. Then mine.

In no time we're split up over two cars with drivers: Jimmy, V., me, and someone named Zaor in the Mercedes up front, and the rest behind it. Above my eyes throbs a pain that had been waiting there for this most inconvenient of moments. It almost seems as if we've been deliberately lured into Grozny to get all miserable and confused. Our sense of direction is at a loss. V. can take us to any arbitrary hideout, we won't be able to put anyone on his track, ever.

He doesn't speak English. Zaor is an interpreter but doesn't have to do much. V. is not a talker. From where I'm sitting I can get a good look at him. The interior lights of the Mercedes are on, I don't know why, maybe he wants to get a good look at us too. His fingernails are smooth and strong. No rings. His beard shows the gray of hair that once was black. There's nothing spurious about him. I know he killed people, but I'm prepared to believe he had to. As my headache keeps throbbing, I tell myself to stay alert. Within the confines of this nuthouse everyone seems normal.

We need to go past an iron hatch and down a ladder. V. has led us to a bomb shelter. This will be our guest room for the next two days. That's fine, I don't need windows, don't want to look at what is no longer there outside. And there's no sound of helicopters down here. They give us food and drink. V. is a Muslim, we know the rules and heed the traditions. Jimmy hardly takes anything.

"Aren't you hungry?" I ask.

Inside and outside there are Chechens standing guard. I can hear them speaking in Vainakh dialect. I start to concentrate on what is about to come. We know why we've been invited. Five weeks earlier, we spoke to V. in England.

There is oil in the Caspian Sea bed. Western oil companies, their Russian and Caucasian partners, and the governments involved have been waging a fight for years over the course of the pipelines. Ten different routes are being disputed, with every country doing its best to shepherd the oil over its own territory. So they can levy taxes. Profitable and easily earned.

The Russian Federation determined the rules of the game for a long time. That way, it had at its disposal 2.1 billion barrels of oil per year, half of which was meant for export. From the Tengiz Field alone, owned by Chevron and Mobil, each year 105 million barrels of crude oil flow from Baku over Grozny to Novorossiysk, the Russian refinery city near the Black Sea. From there on, oil goes across the entire globe.

Chechnya used to be big in refinery. There was a time when the country produced seven hundred thousand barrels a day; half of the Caucasus' total oil production. After the war, the amount of barrels produced dropped from sixty-five hundred to five hundred a day: refinery specialists had fled the country, workers had become soldiers, and about six hundred miles of pipeline had been blown up, by all warring parties.

The Russians sabotaged the lines with equal force because they refused to pay a toll to Chechnya from the moment it declared itself independent in 1991. They still considered the area as Russian and, consequently, saw the pipeline under Grozny as Russian property. The "debt" to Chechnya amounted to five-point-five million dollars.

Then Chechen gangsters started tapping crude oil from the pipeline and sold it below the Russian price. Inevitably, the latter bombed a part of the line used for tapping and in reply the rebels destroyed the other pipes. And so it went on. A regular breach in the line costs about twenty-five tons of oil a day; out here the Russians sometimes lost five hundred tons a day.

Soon the Russians decided to make the best of a bad bargain and started exchanging oil for "surveillance" of the pipeline by gangsters. This lasted until the Kremlin got the idea to permanently loop the pipeline around Chechnya. They made a bypass on the Tikhoretsk pipe in Baku so that, from then on, the oil could flow over Dagestan to Novorossiysk.

And this is where V. came into the picture. He has founded a company to try to establish a new pipeline in Chechnya. But then he'll need investors. Jimmy can take care of that, he knows the right people.

Zaor translates what V. is saying: "If we can manage to build a line from the Tengiz Field to Baku, over Grozny and Tbilisi, we can eliminate the federation. From Baku, a connection with the Mediterranean Sea can easily be made through Turkey. Via Armenia and Iran the oil could even be directed to the Persian Gulf. That way we get around Russia and Chechnya finally receives the money it has a right to. Once we're up and running, we can also exploit the supply underneath Grozny."

Jimmy becomes interested again. I can see dollar signs in his eyes. We talk about the investors that V. is looking for, the routes that are already there. V. gets the map. He unwrinkles the paper with his wrists. I see that he's wearing two watches.

I fight against the image of Pavel looking at his watch, at the edge of the pit. Had the watch been slow, would the horse still be alive? I think of the square, of the vanished Grozny circus, of home, of Martin.

All of a sudden Jimmy doesn't want to talk anymore. V. nods. There is a place where we can sleep. Zaor leads us to it.

Jimmy has the room next to mine. We're standing alone in a hallway, with the doorknobs in our hands. He mumbles that he has pain: somewhere below his shoulder blades. And a fever. He yawns, wobbles into his room, and closes the door. I'm so tired that what I should be asking doesn't even occur to me.

The next morning Jimmy falls ill. Dangerously ill. A doctor arrives from somewhere out of the bombarded streets of Grozny. He diagnoses severe pneumonia. I confer with Zaor.

The doctor can provide antibiotics, but really, Jimmy should get out of here as soon as possible. Perhaps we can arrange for a helicopter to take him to the hospital in Ankara. I nod. After that I want to be alone with the patient. I wake him up.

"Jimmy," I say, "what do you want me to do? Shall I stay here to find out what V. wants, and discuss the terms?"

Jimmy shakes his head.

"Trust me," I say. "We've been over this deal so many times, I know what you want. Ten percent of the exploitation profits, for five years; minimum profit determined per contract. I can do this on my own."

"V. doesn't want to do business with a woman." He coughs.

"We have to earn back your lifestyle of the past few weeks," I say sharply. Before Jimmy answers, I tap the cover of his bed. "This afternoon you'll be in Ankara," I say. "I'll join you as soon as I've finished here."

"Maria," he says, coughing, "ten percent, no less."

* * *

V. and Zaor are waiting for me. I say that we can resume the meeting now and ask Zaor for the feasibility study of the project. He translates my request. V. looks back calmly and speaks. Zaor nods a lot. He says that V. wants to adjourn the meeting because he can imagine that Mr. Liu would rather have his secretary accompany him on his trip to Turkey.

"I'm his acting manager, not his secretary."

He doesn't translate but replies immediately, "Oh! Acting manager? Good, good, but your boss is ill, seriously ill."

I smile.

"Precisely. Seriously ill. Therefore it is fortunate that I am still here to fulfill Mr. Liu's engagement. Mr. Liu would be profoundly astonished to learn that both of you refuse to consider his manager as a valid business partner. Mr. V. and I can still reach an agreement this very day."

V. stands up and leaves the room. The interpreter goes with him. I stay behind and wait until the gentlemen have agreed that the simple fact of having a vagina doesn't sit in the way of a transaction totaling more than a hundred million dollars.

They give me the feasibility study. I spend the ensuing hours reading and asking questions. I inquire about the risks of leakage and oil theft by gangsters. Crude oil with a high sulfur level affects the pipes. Oil from the Tengiz Field contains a lot of sulfur.

I let them explain to me who will make the line operational, maintain and run it, and why the investor shouldn't fear an intervention on the federation's behalf.

The Russians won't interfere with the plan, V. assures me:

they get a small percentage of the exploitation profit and the promise that the pipeline will be kept free of rebels by V. and his army. The Russians have already consented to the plan and to leaving this pipeline to the Chechens by way of reparation. Besides, V. himself is the biggest investor in the plan and that inspires my confidence.

Much later—Jimmy must be in Ankara by now—I get to the cash flow diagram. I have to stay focused. No daylight in twenty-four hours saps your strength. As do twenty cups of sugar tea. Normally Jimmy and I do this together. All estimates and tenders seem in order.

I take a breath for the next round.

V. remains remarkably calm for someone who's in need of money. I can't catch him at making a gesture that gives away his emotions. It's because we're talking with the human screen of Zaor in between.

I ask V. how much he wants to pay Jimmy.

He offers a profit margin of 9 percent for five years, of a minimum profit to be determined, in exchange for investors from China. The percentage is almost high enough. I hardly need to say anything in order to close the deal. But there seems to be room for more. Actually, I want to beat Jimmy to the punch. So I say that I'm willing to consider it, but only if they throw in weapon supplies to Chechnya for us as well.

He shakes his head. Zaor says that they won't handicap their standard suppliers.

"Your weapons are coming from Russia," I say. "No Chinese investor will put money in your pipeline as long as that's the case."

V.'s face is still rigid, but grows a little whiter. He studies his pen and when he looks up at me, I fear that I've overplayed my hand.

"He says that you're not the first woman with the eyes of a deer but the claws of a wolf. He has no say in weapon supplies to Chechnya or Ingushetia. That is up to the president and the general."

"Nobody knows the president and the general better than your boss," I reply against my better judgment. "Despite their power, your boss is the only one who can decide whether the pipeline will be built with Chinese money or not." I start packing up my briefcase, slowly.

V. asks for a moment of patience, he needs to make a phone call. I wait, having used up all my tricks.

Jimmy would have been satisfied with a part of the profit from the pipeline. We never talked about weapon supplies. I punish him for not daring to trust me. Maybe I'll regret that in the morning. But now I want to see money.

Then Zaor and V. come to tell me that V. wants to continue our talk. I smile. V. smiles back. He's unaware of my relief.

We quickly agree on the details. Jimmy gets his 10 percent exploitation profit, determined for five years, and is allowed to deliver ammunition and machine guns for seven million dollars.

V. offers me one more night's stay in the bunker. I decline.

Midnight. There's a jeep ready, with two Chechens in Russian uniforms. I dress up as a soldier again. V. laughs when he sees me. He whispers something to Zaor. He nods but doesn't translate. When I make a move to get in, he stops me for a moment.

"V. wants to know how you liked Grozny."

This surprises me. V. sees this and quickly says something to Zaor.

"He wants you to know that we won't let ourselves be chased away. In spite of any devastation." V. shakes my hand in goodbye.

"I have a request." My voice falters. "About six miles north of Koelary there is a dead horse lying in a mud pool. The pool is on the land of a farm with a dead woman and three dead children inside. It would be great if you could remove the bodies and the cadaver."

V. nods kindly, while Zoar translates everything. I know that he won't meet my request. And he knows that I can't be grieving for more than a day about what is happening in this country. But as a polite expression of mutual concern, posing the question and providing the affirmative answer will do.

Having landed in Ankara, I call Jimmy right away. I'm surprised to hear Victor pick up. He's supposed to be in Thailand, Very Far Away.

He jabbers that he spent the past ten days in Amsterdam, at our office: "Doing chores for Jimmy."

As soon as Jimmy called, he set out for Turkey.

I want to speak to Jimmy.

"No, Maria, he's just having a rest. He can manage fine without you, you know!"

I feel a rising urge to kill, but think: *I can chop off his head but he'll just grow two new ones instead.*

Finally I get to speak to Jimmy.

"What 'chores' in the office?" I inquire suspiciously.

"Thanks, Maria, I'm feeling a lot better," he says.

I decide to bring this up again when he's back on his feet. Dammit, this conversation isn't going like I had imagined it at all. For the sake of formality, Jimmy asks how it went. I tell him about the deal. How splendid it went, for a woman.

"Well, Maria, that sounds nice."

Nice? Whose expenditures did I fucking earn back in that shithole Grozny? How sick does he still feel? I ask when I can drop by. He says I don't have to "with Victor here."

Everything I should have done differently doesn't strike me until I put down the phone.

I take the plane to the Netherlands, sick of Grozny, of guns, of Jimmy and everything connected to him.

In Utrecht I call Martin. Not home. I go over my voice mail and hear that Mark has left me a message. Three times. I'm not in the mood to talk about the company, it's just that Mark never calls. I dial his number. He picks up immediately.

"Maria, I got fired five days ago."

When he repeats it, I realize what he's saying. What happened, for God's sake?

He tells me how Victor called him to his office. He thought it was just going to be about covering up expenses again.

"But I sensed right away that he wanted to get me out of the way. He said that Jimmy was tired of me, an accountant acting like an educator. I could leave right away. I tried to reach Jimmy, but he wasn't in. I thought you were in Holland, so I left a message. I had no idea that you two were away."

I ask if I can do anything.

"Could you talk to Jimmy? This is crazy!"

I promise.

I want to put some heart into him but, because of the shock, I can't think of what to say. We say goodbye.

I'm about to hang up when he says, "Maria, I hate to say this, but Victor also said something else. He said, 'Staal is next.' I'm really sorry, Maria, but that's how he said it."

CHAPTER 10

Evening. I'm in bed with Nella, dressed. Her hand is resting on my neck. We're lying on our sides. Facing each other, for now. If I turn around, I'll fall on the floor. If she turns around, I'll be uncovered. This has always puzzled me: even when you're bundled up you still get cold in areas that aren't under the cover.

She's wide awake. There's always a scent of the outdoors around her, soil, wood. That deep black hair. Not flowers. Trees. Saplings.

"Are you all right?"

She doesn't know that she's breathing on my eyelid. Each time a cool breeze. If I want to avoid it, I'll have to lift my head and tilt it.

I told her that we'd better put out the lamp. That otherwise we'll be lying open-eyed till morning. I told her not to think about that bad dream anymore. That I'm with her now. I tried to say that in a loving and comforting way. But she's only keeping still because I sounded impatient. I know how hard she's trying to do everything I say, keeping her eyes closed. As long as I promise to stay.

I think: *When will she be able to be her own source of comfort; how old do they need to be?*

Usually I'm good at this but now it's gotten too late. I don't really need to sleep but when I close my eyes I drift away.

I have to get back to Martin, downstairs. There was a documentary that he wanted us to watch together, about an experimental housing development in Buenos Aires.

"Look at that!" he said. "For a complicated design like that you need a construction wizard. And someone who knows a lot about reinforced concrete."

I didn't think it looked that complex but I was willing to go along with it, as long as it was on the TV and he was sitting next to me, and as long as there was red wine on the table and a plate of cheese to snack on, placed there specially for me, enough of everything for an hour with him.

"You have to go to sleep," I whisper.

Her little hand shifts to my shoulder. The spot on my neck where it used to be feels cold. The arm I'm lying on is tingling violently.

There is more, I think. More than just that bad dream.

"What are you worried about?" I ask.

Her fingers pinch my skin rhythmically.

"That they'll see me at the fair. And that they'll bully me too."

"Because you're there with Sjanna?"

I feel how she nods.

Her principal would have had his pedagogical criticism at the ready. I just want her to sleep.

"Then we'll do it here first. We haven't asked Sjanna yet, so everything is possible."

I feel how she calms down. Stupid of me not to think of that earlier. You try very hard during the day but so much goes wrong that you have to make it right again at bedtime.

She talks on to postpone sleep, asks in a yawn, "Did you ever get scared? When you were as old as I am?"

I could reassure her. I could say, "Of course, honey. Every kid your age does."

In fact, I started to get scared much later. When I was a lot older. Really scared. The kind that gives chills to your mother. At an age when your mother isn't with you anymore. What seemed bearable at work was insufferable in dreams. It pressed so hard onto my chest that I felt like drowning.

"Of course, honey," I say, "every kid your age does."

"And did it pass?"

Her voice drops out. I can hear how she drifts away. Her fingertips slide down my arm.

I wake up. It's the middle of the night. I try to sneak from under Nella's cover. I move as slowly as I can, but I'm sore, lack subtlety. I stop now and then, listening to hear if it's still quiet.

I end up on the edge of the bed and let my eyes get used to the dark. I stand up and turn around. As I'm gently fixing the bedclothes again, my hands follow the lines of her body. She's sleeping on her left side. Her eyelashes are long and steep, you can tell during the day, but not now, because it's so dark. Yet I know.

I know that the closet, covered in stickers, is just three steps behind me. Six steps to the left: curtain, window, wall. I find the corner of her desk by touch and my foot bumps into some plastic building blocks. I'm mindful about every step, as if I'm walking through a minefield.

I'm standing in the hallway and run my thumb over the wall a few times. I'm looking for the spot that once had a hole. If you don't know where it is, then you won't see it. The water pipes had to be laid bare because of a leak. When everything had dried I plastered the hole. Layer by layer I applied the filler.

Underneath it sits a note: *This is Our House.*

No one else knows. Shouldn't we take the note with us, so that it doesn't bring bad luck to the next owner?

There's some beer in the fridge. And I've found the cheese snacks again. I sit down at the kitchen table and put the cheese snacks in front of me. I pop the cap off the bottle, put it to my lips, and let the beer flow. I wipe a ring of moisture from the table with my fist. I eat three cheese snacks. I blow the crumbs off the top, onto the floor. One bit sticks to the spot where the stain was.

When I open the second bottle, the cap falls to the floor. I can hear where it bounces off to, sweep the kitchen floor with my foot.

I hear Martin come down the stairs. He doesn't switch on the light.

"Eva Maria?"

* * *

He's naked. Naked, sleepy man in the kitchen, wearing glasses. With his back turned against me, he pours himself a glass of wine. His buttocks are whiter than his calves and his calves are whiter than the moon.

"How's your eye?"

"Fine."

He points at Nella's room, right above our heads.

"The two of you were sleeping," he says.

"Was it okay, that program?" I ask.

"Well, it was interesting to see how some people won't allow any obstacle or technical impossibility to get in their way."

"I'm sorry that I missed the bulk of it."

"I taped it for you."

He doesn't understand that it's not about that at all.

I feel tired all of a sudden, dog-tired.

He says that he'll clean up. That I should go ahead upstairs.

So I do.

I am asleep before he gets in next to me.

CHAPTER 11

I hear how Jimmy opens the refrigerator door and slams it shut again. The office is deserted. It'll be Christmas in a week. Since my trip to Grozny, every silence has become a void that swallows me entirely. I crave for ordinary people, but the only one I see is Jimmy.

With a bottle of champagne under his armpit he wheels his chair next to mine. He flings a box of yesterday's take-out sushi onto my desk. I uncork the bottle without a pop. We eat out of the box. Drink out of the bottle. Jimmy collects the small plastic fish filled with soy sauce. He has a score of them in his drawer, next to all the free business-class slippers and a bag of cigar bands. He doesn't use any of it but doesn't toss it either.

Because there's nothing to celebrate, the champagne doesn't go down well.

"It was either this or Campari," says Jimmy.

In the glass wall of the office we see ourselves floating above the city. The two of us having dinner in the sky. The people down below are riding the bus through the wet snow or making their way from store to store. I sent Martin a postcard. No reply.

Jimmy and I need to talk but we don't seem to get there. He knows me, and I know him. It's been much too long. We can't listen to each other without getting irritated, and want the other to know that. How long does it take before you get to this stage? You notice when it's too late to do anything about it.

After dinner he moves his chair a quarter of a turn. His left hand is resting on his leg. I know what's coming: he grabs my ear—his hand smells of fish and seaweed—and when he springs back, there's a dollar coin between thumb and index finger. *Table magic.* He's a star at it. He blows onto the coin and lets it disappear in his right fist. With a grin he opens both hands. Empty. I never see how he does it. This is also how he makes our money disappear.

He yells, "Talk? Why?" Thinks it can wait until summer, in the sun, by the canal. In the meantime he's picking hundred-dollar bills out of my hair.

"Child's play," he says, "I know a lot more difficult tricks." That fit of pneumonia has made him short of breath. I miss his cigars, he quit smoking.

"And we *will* talk by the canal this summer," I say, pushing away his hand. "About boats, cars, the Beatles, whatever you like."

We live in an unsteady balance. He can't do without me, I guess, but the day he admits that, it'll be over and out.

The conversation should be about money, especially the lack thereof. About Mark the accountant, who got fired. About Staal, who "will be next," according to Victor.

In fact, the conversation should really be about Victor. More than ever about Victor, who I hope is cheating on Jimmy with someone else. I hope this someone has AIDS, and that they discover it timely in Jimmy, but that it's too late for poor Victor.

Jimmy chatters on about the FIM-92E Stinger and compares it to the Chinese QW-2, he talks about the people he met in Paris at a weapons expo and about the plane trip he'll be making shortly to Hong Kong, and that he's thrilled to be celebrating Christmas in the air with May and Li-An of Cathay Pacific, who always pamper him like a baby. He has his own seat, 1A, and can already tell that the plane will be as good as empty.

Then he says, "Maria, you look like hell lately." It doesn't sound as if he cares what's going on, more as if he hates the fact of having to look at it.

I say, "Is it true that you gave Victor permission to fire Mark?"

He flattens the bills, puts them in his inside pocket, and presses his fingertips together. I wait.

Then he says that he wanted to spare me this, too painful.

"I didn't want to trouble you with this, Maria, but Mark did some things for which he had no permission."

"I'm supposed to know these things; why wasn't I informed?" I say.

I tell him to explain everything, right now, and I also want to know why the hell he let Victor take care of it.

He says it had to be done immediately because otherwise it would have cost a lot more, "and we were in Chechnya at the time."

He says, "We'll talk about it after Christmas. It almost seems as if you don't believe me!"

He conjures up a present out of nowhere. It says *Givenchy* on the glossy white paper. Jesus! I gently undo the black ribbon. It's a cashmere houndstooth coat, haute couture. He takes it out of my hands, holds it up. The coat slips over my shoulders nicely. I look in the window. How does Jimmy know my size, my taste?

"Stand still, you. It's a perfect fit."

He puts my collar up and drapes my hair over my shoulders. Shit, I really should prepare myself for things like this to happen.

"For Grozny, Maria. Why don't you take some time off? You made a great effort, take my Goldwing Card, you can be in Barbados by tomorrow, and take what's-his-name with you."

Hit the beach with Martin. Jimmy's paying.

"Sorry that I doubted you," I stammer.

He has to go because Victor's waiting for him downstairs, he's driving him to Rotterdam Airport. When he gets into the elevator he waves and smiles.

I want to stay still for a very long time. But after only three counts I'm dialing Mark's number. I ask him if he's kept a shadow administration. And if I can have a look at it.

"Jimmy isn't doing too well, Maria."

I say that I know that. And that I'm coming over right away.

After I've listened to Mark and studied his books I see two options: either I try to freeze two of Jimmy's bank accounts and close a huge deal as soon as possible, no matter what, no matter who, or I hand in my resignation and gun down Victor on the way home.

That Jimmy's lying to me is not new; that he's risking the company to be able to afford his lover is.

Mark tells me there's going to be a private pre-tender meeting, on January 5 somewhere in New York. After some digging we find out the name of the Pakistani who distributed the tenders to four dealers. It's Azhar. I know that name. The meeting concerns weapons for the police and the army. I think it's strange that we haven't been asked for an offer. I mean: Pakistan, it's been our business partner for years!

When I call Karachi I'm told that Azhar did send us a tender. "But Jimmy didn't feel he had anything for it, Maria."

I hang up. That Jimmy decides to squander our money on boys and casinos is bad. That he refuses to earn it back is unforgivable.

Freezing the two accounts appears to be impossible. The bank wants to see some authorization.

I manage to get a seat on a fully booked flight to New York for January 2. I also get hold of Azhar. We're new to each other. He knows Jimmy, but not me. A handicap. He says that the registration date has passed. I ask him when the tenders are due. January 7. "But that is of no importance to you."

I explain that Jimmy's refusal was a mistake. I mention our fast deliveries, our low prices, our guaranteed quality. The silence tells me that it's time for my act. I mean the act that earns him money for hearing me out. He bites. The amount for which he's willing to let us submit our delayed tender to him will be coming out of his own pocket, I'll sneak it into the offer I'm going to send him later on.

I ask who else is in the race. Again he hesitates. Again he wants money. Fine. He gives me four names. I pay up four times. Three colleagues I know quite well. The fourth only by reputation: Sulleyman from Louisiana. He's someone that Jimmy and I prefer to avoid, but Pakistan seems to be doing business with everyone nowadays. In an agitated mood, Jimmy once declared that Sulleyman was behind the bullet letters for Shen-li and Suze, as well as behind the attempt on his life in Pakistan.

"This hole in my face is Sulleyman's work! Pissed off about a few goddamn centrifuge parts!"

I realized straightaway that he was talking bull; Sulleyman is cunning, not stupid. You're better off being attacked by a Mississippi alligator than you are when closing a deal with this asshole.

I work through the nights, I work through the Christmas holidays, Jimmy can't suspect a thing.

Martin doesn't call. Whenever I sleep, I dream about us. We have a dog together but it dies. We live in a house together but the roof leaks. We have to be somewhere but we get lost.

The last day of the year I call him up.

Yes, of course, he got my card. Nice. Yep, uh-huh, he's fine. The conversation saturates with still longer pauses. I hear a woman whisper something, then hear Martin put his hand over the receiver. I ask no questions. Not about her name, not about her looks, not about whether she is what he really wants. I say goodbye and hang up.

The 747 is grounded. Broken-winged. Nothing to do but wait. The old lady next to me strikes up a conversation. She's visiting her granddaughter in New York for the second time.

"Impressive," she says.

"New York?" I ask in my politest voice, but what I think is: Grozny.

She's talking about the famous museum with the barosaurus skeleton, near the park.

I dream away. Imagine that I let myself be locked in, so that I could watch that dino all night long and think of objects in the ground: red and brown pottery, petrified bones, a child from the Shang Dynasty with a small wooden block in her mouth on which her date of death is carved, the half-digested fruit in the stomach of a mastodon . . .

We need to transfer to get to New York via Heathrow. I help the old lady and fall asleep next to her on the other plane.

In my sixth month of working for Jimmy an African general sent us a tender for a consignment. Jimmy and I called up middlemen and manufacturers for days in a row and calculated our offer.

Then Jimmy took me to a club somewhere in Sussex. The owner was expecting us. She asked, "Mr. and Mrs. Woh?" Jimmy nodded. I had never heard him use a fake name before. We had to keep on walking until we got to a stuffy room. Men were sitting around a table. The competition. They introduced themselves to me, not unkindly, and continued talking, smoking, and drinking.

I recognized an Englishman named Barillion, the German twin brothers Scholl, and a Pole named Jabukowski. Jimmy put me in a chair, a little in the back. "Shut up, watch, and listen, Maria."

A balding man stood up and opened the meeting. He looked around the circle and briefly discussed the African tender: "As you all know, the order consists of three parts. Are all of you willing to deliver each part?"

Everyone nodded, including Jimmy. I didn't get that. I thought that only the simulators interested him.

The chairman continued, "This is a nice deal, let's not try to get in each other's way. We'd better make a few sensible agreements."

He suggested they follow "the usual procedure." This turned out to be a price comparison, in order to protect everyone from making an offer that was simply too sharp.

Everyone wrote down his price on a folded piece of paper and put it in front of him on the table. The chairman collected them. He read them out loud: amounts, including the names.

The German twins had the lowest price. The chairman now referred to the brothers as "rightful claimants": they could supply the weapons to the African general. The rest refrained from delivery. They agreed not to lower their prices, not even at the request of the client. Next, everyone's offer was raised by 10 percent of the German price. The twins, in their turn, had to pay 8 percent of that amount to the remaining contestants as a token of gratitude for the exclusive rights.

"That's called 'compensation,'" Jimmy explained afterward.

Then everyone got up, shook hands, each took his own note and left.

It's three in the afternoon, it's freezing bricks. I'll have to buy a warmer coat, a good excuse to go shopping.

Sitting in the taxi from Kennedy Airport I once again drive past the biggest cemetery I've ever seen. Shreds of ticker tape from New Year's Eve fill up the gutters on Times Square. I ignore the city. To the hotel first. I've still got two days until my pretender meeting.

My plan is to ask my four competitors for "preference" straightaway: the right to take over the order. I have to speak with every dealer in private before the meeting. Sulleyman is last in line, that's all I've come up with so far.

When did Jimmy get like this? I was there but didn't notice anything. I also thought I knew Martin.

I used to wonder why those "compensations" were never recorded in the books.

He waved my question aside: "Pfff, that money only exists on the scratch pad, Maria."

Then he explained: Every agreement is canceled out by a new one, the money is always passed on to the next deal, the amount never stays the same for long. Everyone keeps track of his own list. Once a year we settle the accounts.

"We are received by two retired dealers. Everyone hands in his list. We greenhorns have fun while they work everything out. At the end of the day everyone pays off his remaining debt to the others. In cash."

My tender mentions fragmentation grenades: DPICMs, 103 pounds each. Meant for killing Hindus and Sikhs. Encased in the ice of the Kargil Pass, in Jammu and Kashmir, at a height of twenty thousand feet, are fragments with bits of heart muscle and battle dress stuck to them. This is the demarcation line between Pakistan and India.

That same night, I call up all four competitors and arrange meetings. Two for tomorrow, two for the day after.

The youngest is Harry Chi. I meet him in the afternoon at Wollman Rink in the park. A Taiwanese on ice skates. He clomps ahead of me, up the stands. Skyscrapers block the sun. We're in for some snow.

I say that I would like to supply the entire tender, alone. He takes a swig from his energy drink and shakes his head. His hair grows straight up, unlike Jimmy's.

"No, this tender is mine."

I look at him. He doesn't care about the order. He's acting. I used to have trouble reading body language. But now I have about seen it all. In ten seconds I'll know how much money it will take to change Harry Chi's mind. There we have it: He still had a small supply of Kalashnikovs that he was planning to work into the offer. Can I compete against that? He names his numbers. I name a price. He refuses indignantly. We struggle on, for a few thousand dollars less or more. The ice rink is getting deserted.

"Harry," I say with a sigh, "come on, I'm getting cold. You don't have the logistics to handle this order and the others have already given me preference."

I'm bluffing. I haven't talked to anyone else yet. But he believes me. We make a deal. We shake hands.

One down, three to go.

I want snow in the summer, not now. I hurry into a department store to get myself some pug boots and an overcoat, just before my meeting with Gregorius Brand, the competitor from Austria. I linger for a moment in front of a rack with couture lingerie. Then head on to the shoes department.

After a while someone taps my shoulder.

"Miss?" the saleswoman gasps. "Your account has been settled."

She thrusts a small bag into my hands. Containing a set of very expensive lingerie. She's gone before I can ask a question.

My eyes scan for Martin, Jimmy, Santa Claus, but find no one.

* * *

A little while later I'm sitting with my little bag at Guastavino's, in upper midtown. Gregorius Brand and I are having crab. Brand is more difficult to read than Harry Chi but every time we did business, he cut us some space.

"There's an African tender coming up," he says. "Perhaps Jimmy could take a step back then."

"Take a step back? According to my notes you still owe him a million, Gregorius."

Does he think I'm stupid? Now he'll probaby move on to the amount of the compensation.

"Then we'll have to up the ante a little," he says, "otherwise I'm not following your lead."

Then he asks where Jimmy is. How he's doing. I don't get into specifics.

He says, "Watch yourself, Maria. There's talk going around about Jimmy. They don't take him as seriously as they used to anymore. He should be glad he still has you. We know how much you earned for him in Chechnya. And how. But does he know?"

I make a quick joke. He laughs. I ask him if, by any chance, he saw me shopping in the afternoon. He doesn't know what I'm talking about, shakes his head.

"Oh." I smile. "Too bad."

At night Shen-li calls me on my cell. He thinks he's calling Utrecht at eleven in the morning. I sit up straight in bed. Is this about Jimmy?

Shen-li says, "Money has been deposited into my account. Jimmy told me, 'You'll be getting a Christmas present,' but this is absurd, disturbing even."

I wince at the amount. Dammit, and here I am trying to plug the holes through which daddy-dearest's money disappears! I ask Shen-li not to touch the money until I've found out more about it. He won't. Neither will his sister. He asks what New York is like.

"Cold."

He makes me promise to have fun. I think about the lingerie in my hotel trash can. We hang up. It's already too late when I realize that Jimmy can't know that I'm here. Shit, forgot to tell him!

Morning. Even colder than yesterday. On the way to a coffee-house in Upper West to meet with Renzo the Mexican. But it's his assistant sitting at the bar, Clarita. No Renzo in sight.

The unpleasant surprise is mutual. She was expecting Jimmy.

Clarita resembles a bunch of flowers that has been kept for too long. I think she fucks Renzo but also his clients—and competitors—whenever he tells her to. Jimmy always claims that he never aswered her advances but they get along very well. Her mouth is too wide, her boobs sit too high, and she's ignorant about weapons.

"Clarita!" I say gleefully. We kiss the air above each other's cheeks.

This is to become a conversation in which Clarita concedes something to me. She knows this. I'm the one who asked for this meeting. She leans back. I tell my story. Explain that everyone has already said yes. She smiles.

"No," she says. She enjoys, savors the word, and repeats, "No, Renzo and me are out. We want to supply, ourselves. The last time we came knocking on Jimmy's door for preference, he also refused to play ball."

She means a small delivery to Croatia. Peanuts. I try to talk her around, try to assess if there is still something to be got. She gives me nothing, no direction, no leads. This is how I'll have to go into the meeting tomorrow: two for, one against. And I haven't even talked to Sulleyman.

When I get up, she says, "I don't understand why you're going through all this trouble for Jimmy. First Chechnya, now this."

"I thought you were so crazy about him," I say in a silvery voice.

She grins. "He wasn't gay back then."

You could always complain to Martin that you weren't smart and sexy enough. He'd pep you up. He was good at that. Because he meant what he said. Jimmy always kicks you while you're down. Until you're so furious that you're set on proving him wrong. The one was my wailing wall, the other my punching bag. I could use both right now.

Everyone says that Sulleyman probably was a bug in all of his previous lifetimes, something slimy that crawls and waits under a damp rock. He won't speak to me until late in the evening, his secretary informs me, in the restaurant of a fancy nightclub.

In the back of the taxi I think of Jimmy's eye. Whoever fired that shot hit more than an eye. Everything has changed since that morning in Pakistan. If I convince myself that Sulleyman is responsible, I might have a chance tonight.

* * *

He's calm and considerate. We look for a table in the back, where we can talk at ease. I say something funny without knowing it, and he laughs out loud. I feel myself slip, never have I fallen so quickly, so deeply for a man. He doesn't flirt. Doesn't touch me. I listen to him. It's his voice. It sounds like timeless music, like water. Utterly confused, I try to concentrate.

He nods perceptively when I solicit preference. I lie that all the others have already conceded. He asks why I'm here without Jimmy. I scan for sarcasm and suspicion in that question but find none. He says, "I will grant you preference. But there is no need to protect Jimmy. He doesn't have anything to fear from me. He's been digging his own grave for a long time. Everyone can see it. We know how you fended for yourself in Chechnya. Jimmy can't count on our support any longer. Clean this mess up one more time and come work for me. Have you tasted the wine yet?"

I stare at him, motionless, as he raises his glass without batting his eyelids. I should go to the bathroom and run some cold water over my wrists, recuperate some of that contempt for him. I get up and murmur an excuse.

"Maria," he says compellingly, "ask yourself what good he is to you."

I nod. Not in answer to his question but to the way my name sounded coming from his mouth.

We say nothing in the cab on the way to my hotel. His offer is on the table. I need time.

"About the meeting, tomorrow," Sulleyman ponders. "I'm chairman. If Renzo says no, it'll be tough. Especially for you."

He doesn't move when I get out. I have one leg outside the cab when I say, rather recklessly, "I'll never wear it. I got rid of it."

I am hoping that my remark will throw him off as much as it did Brand yesterday. It has to.

"Understandable." He smiles. "But it was worth a laugh."

I get out, perfectly beside myself. He closes the car door. The snow crackles where the cab accelerates.

A warehouse on the crossing of Chinatown and Little Italy. Cardboard boxes everywhere, with star anise and fortune cookies packed on top of raw uncut opium. Harry Chi, Gregorius Brand, Renzo, and I are sitting around the table, with Sulleyman as chairman. He says that we are gathered here for a Pakistani tender. To make sure no one miscalculated.

He asks, "Is everyone willing to supply?"

They nod. All of them! Closed ranks. I ask for permission to speak.

I say, "Listen up, Jimmy Liu and I have the 'oldest right' to Pakistan. Everyone at this table has received help from us in the past year. You, Gregorius, I expect you to back me up."

Brand taps his nose with his finger, to fake ponderation. At last he says he's willing to renounce delivery in exchange for a "decent compensation." Sulleyman and Harry Chi say nothing. I look at Renzo. He shakes his head. "Sorry, Maria, this is our deal."

I ask Harry Chi if he can explain why he did agree to go along at first.

He says, "You assured me that the others had come around. When they have, you'll get my preference."

They play poker with the cards against their chests. "Only when the fish decides to be caught, you catch the fish," is what Jimmy always says. Patience. I look at Sulleyman, who hasn't said anything at all. Not a word about giving me preference or not. He looks back, amused. He's testing me. How callous is Staal, exactly?

"Come on, Maria," says Harry Chi, "we don't have all day."

"Yeah," says Brand. "This is not how it works."

One chance, give me one goddamn chance, I've watched this game being played many times. I try to think fast. I'm sure that I can win over Harry and Gregorius. Sulleyman is acting shady. Renzo refuses.

I look at Sulleyman and say, "I want to have a word in private with Renzo."

"You and me first," he says softly.

"No," I say. "First Renzo. In the hallway."

"Half a million," Renzo insists. "And I don't want to see you or Jimmy at that deal for Georgia in May. In addition, you'll see to a decent compensation, in due time, for this delivery."

I want to punch him in the face. He's fleecing me. I have no choice.

The others are waiting inside. Then Sulleyman steps into the hallway. He sits down, in his nice suit, on a crate, his feet on the concrete floor. I stand up.

He says, "Come work for me and you have your preference for Pakistan."

"No, Sulleyman, you already promised to give me preference yesterday. I'm keeping you to your word."

He shakes his head. "My word? You must have misunderstood. I didn't promise you anything."

I say, "You can get a hundred thousand dollars. Not a cent more. Chi, Brand, and Renzo are on board, that's what I pay them for. They'll drop you the next time if you back out now and blow up their deal."

He knows I'm right. He must do what I want.

He gets up and takes one step forward. "I really got the impression that Jimmy didn't have an appetite for this tender. Then yesterday you started bothering me. What's up with that? Do you two know what the other is up to?"

I laugh at him. "Jimmy changed his mind. It happens."

"You're not there yet." He smiles. "The amount of the compensation is yet to be determined."

Do the gentlemen grant me the order now? Everyone nods approvingly. Except Sulleyman, he's polishing his nails on his lapels.

Renzo asks what quotation price I'm planning to offer to the client.

I know what I'm up against: One by one they'll come down on my rates. Surely I can do better. They want to push up their compensations as much as they can by keeping my price as low as possible. We can't have the Pakistanis think that we're ripping them off.

I know what I have to earn to save Jimmy's company. A simple sum with a tight result. They collectively lower my quotation price. Until Chairman Sulleyman decides that it's enough. Within five minutes we've reached a price that will keep Jimmy alive and the others satisfied. Now it seems as if I needed Sulleyman!

Outside he gives me his business card: "Just in case you get tired of old one-eye, or the other way around. Or just for when you can't sleep."

I put the card away, thinking it's not worth a glance, but his cell phone number jumps out at me. It's promptly chiseled in my memory. He doesn't smile. Raises his hand and leaves. It's night, late.

I enter my hotel room in the dark, leave the lights off. I didn't call Martin and didn't get drunk. I feel my way to the bed.

I could belong entirely and unconditionally to Sulleyman tonight. He would have to say something. Not whisper in the same voice as everyone else. No, in his standard speaking voice, which sears like fire and chills like ice. Scattered words: soft, come, breathe, deeper, Maria, Maria. I fall asleep with my hand between my thighs and his name in my head. Too scant for a dream.

The first morning without snow. Jimmy should be pleased. The only thing he'll have to do is agree to account for the expenses made on this trip.

I leave at two o'clock. Busy packing, I receive a call. Jimmy. Out of courtesy he asks what I'm doing in New York but I hear that he knows already.

"Making money. What else? If I'd wanted to take some time off you'd be calling Barbados right now, wouldn't you?"

Now he's going to chew the fat, nag, feeling passed over, although he won't admit it, of course. Always some bullshit I don't want to hear.

I say, "Can't you just be happy? Can't you think just for once: *Oh, that Maria, here she goes again, getting me out of some deep shit in her spare time, what a great gal?*"

He yells, "Shit? There's no shit! By giving everybody that idea you're screwing things up."

I want to strangle him but ask politely why he refused the

invitation from Pakistan. Even though we're almost bankrupt. Even though we always do business with Pakistan. He says he doesn't want to let on about anything. To me.

"I do, Jimmy!" I scream into the phone. "I just want to let on that it seems as though you're deliberately trying to bring down the company. I don't know why, perhaps spending money is the only thing that still appeals to you."

He snarls at me, asking if I realize that taking action without his permission can get me fired. Right now. On the spot.

Who is he kidding? What will he do without me?

I say measuredly, "I'll just pretend I didn't hear that."

He reacts cool. Tomorrow he'll be back in Amsterdam. We hang up without an appointment, without goodbye.

My blouse is on the bed. The breast pocket contains Sulleyman's business card. I snatch my purse and take out my wallet. The card goes inside.

CHAPTER 12

Mirjam says, "I felt at home right away when I was here last time."

I think: *You're saying that for Sjanna.*

Our daughters walk uncomfortably into the living room, side by side. There they wait for the afternoon to pass by itself, or for the wonder that would make a wonder superfluous.

I talk an awful lot and think of very different things than what I hear myself say. I regret Mirjam saying that she felt at home right away. I don't know, if you don't mean a thing like that, you shouldn't say it. But the funny part is: she carries tea-cups around, fetches spoons to go with them, and chatters to the dachshund as if she's been coming around for years.

I was standing on the kitchen step in front of the linen closet, trunk turned a quarter around. With knees bent lightly and my chin on a pile of sheets I noticed something slipping from the stack with a waft.

In its fall it hit my foot. Something hard.

* * *

I say, "After tea we can bake cookies, if you want."

I manage to pronounce the words "bake cookies" in a natural way, seemingly without effort. Mirjam's face informs me that my laugh is coming across as well. Perhaps because I'm starting to get more and more serious about all of this.

Nella and Sjanna wanted to play hide-and-seek.

"Can we hide anywhere?"

Nella was the one who asked and I said yes.

"Even in the attic?"

"Even in the attic."

"But not in your bedroom, I guess?"

There she can disappear under the bed or in the wardrobe or in the laundry basket.

"Just this once, the bedroom as well."

All of this to show Sjanna how nice we were, how fun it was over here, how sorry we were for everything.

Nice kid, by the way, Sjanna. Doesn't take you long, to see that this is a very nice kid. Does Sjanna know that herself? Or did all that bullying knock her out of it?

I asked Nella to put herself in Sjanna's place: "Look, she's coming over to play. With someone that bullies her. Behind enemy lines. Let's imagine that for a second. One uncomfortable afternoon for you is a nightmare for Sjanna. You can make sure it will be fun. For the both of you, I mean."

I said all of that. I was talking to Nella's shoulder blades. I was talking to myself and right against forty years of insight into human nature.

* * *

I had sensed—even before it fell down—a child slip past behind me but did not know which child and did not know in what direction, in or out. It was more like a flow of air. I wasn't thinking about their game. The palms of my hands were passing over a cupboard shelf at that moment, beyond my power.

"Bake cookies?" says Mirjam. "Sjanna always likes that, don't you, Sjanna?"

Sjanna waits for Nella to nod. Then she nods.

"It's from one of those ready-to-eat boxes," I say. "Cherrybrook Kitchen's Arthur Cookie Mix. With chocolate chips on top. I hope you haven't grown out of them."

Nella shakes her head. Sjanna follows.

Sjanna says, "You only need to add water."

"And butter," says Nella.

"Yes," I say, "but very little."

I look at my daughter, who refuses to be read.

"Do you also eat the leftover chocolate chips?" she asks.

"I save those for my dad," says Sjanna. "Sometimes, when he's at home, he bakes cookies with me. Or apple pie. My dad is very good at apple pie."

"Mine isn't," says Nella.

Mirjam and Sjanna are nodding sympathetically, while I take some empty cups into the kitchen. I pick up the cookie mix and read the instructions. I can do this. It says, "Experience a baking adventure with Arthur," and then what it takes to get there.

Maybe the child was already on its way to the landing, making for the base area in the hallway to touch the stack of cardboard boxes with both hands. Or was it hiding? In here? Under the bed? Did it see anything? Did it understand anything of what had fallen down? Why wasn't I paying attention? A stream of air was all I could remember. And that I turned around with those sheets.

Mirjam is still sitting on the couch. It's not that I want her to leave. Very unlike me; usually I get tired of visitors after an hour.

The girls are playing upstairs. Maybe we won't even have to bake cookies.

I ask if it's a nice job, behind the counter at the hospital. Not the most interesting of questions. Any question will do. As long as we keep talking about her.

"I used to be a nurse," says Mirjam. "In a mission hospital in western Pakistan."

It comes to me as a blow that this conversation is suddenly stealing off, away from the ophthalmology department to a mission hospital in western Pakistan.

"A mission hospital in western Pakistan?"

"Yes. Well, most people draw a blank. No one ever goes to Pakistan. Near Kalat. Close to Afghanistan. Many children. There were shootings in that area. Always have been."

I was turning out the linen closet. A lot of junk: sheets with worn patches, pillow slips with faded flowers, and a pile of washcloths from fifteen years ago. By the time I get rid of something . . . I hadn't visited that shelf in years.

Pent-up, I struggle against the current, digging for a question about something else. It's no use. She keeps on talking.

"I also got to know my husband at that hospital. He was a patient there. He had broken his leg in a car crash."

There is nothing you can do. I nod and calm myself down. And then I realize what she is in fact saying. My own anxieties have kept me from recognizing hers.

"I liked him more than he did me," she says.

I nod. *I understand you*, is what I think. *I understand all of it. And you would understand me. If only you knew me. If only you liked me enough.*

I pulled a pile of sheets from the top shelf. I didn't think of anything. I hold that against myself, looking back.

After a short silence I say that I forgot to get some chicken, too bad, since we're having such a good time, and look at my watch the while. Then she gets up. She briefly puts her hand on her neck and looks at the floor, her shoes. Then she smiles. She walks in front of me.

"Can she ride her bike home alone?" I ask, because there's still so much snow.

So I was pulling a large pile of sheets from the top shelf. A gun slipped from it, my old Glock. It wasn't loaded, it didn't go off, but it tumbled on the deep-pile carpet and stopped in front of our bed.

I lift her jacket from the coat hook, a brown leather jacket with pockets and narrow shoulders. I smell tobacco and ashes. I have to say something now, something nice, because that is the due reward for someone who says that she feels at ease yet doesn't ask for an ashtray.

* * *

*I threw the sheets on top of it, as a reflex. I mean: the thing, the gun,
the Glock, ended up in front of the bed, perhaps right under someone's nose (if she was hiding there, that is). The most that someone
could have thought was,* Something is falling, *and that's it.* Not
even, *And it looks like a gun. Because the sheets were already on
top of it. On top of that thing, the gun.*

Not that it went like that. That simple.

When she's gone I decide to turn out the linen closet in our bedroom. I have just the time to do that. Almost all of it is junk.

While I'm putting everything away something happens that
should never, never happen again.

The children don't notice anything. Thank God they're somewhere else. Besides, Nella knows that I don't like having people
in the bedroom during hide-and-seek. Even when I say yes, I
can, in fact—as far as this is concerned—mean to say no.

CHAPTER 13

I want to sleep. Just have a damned good sleep. But Jimmy and Victor want to hit downtown Hong Kong. After midnight is when all the fun starts, they say. I tag along. Too tired to decipher the name of the joint we end up at.

It's packed. A Chinese trio is playing something that is supposed to pass off as jazz. A bunch of Americans roar at a glassy-eyed girl leaning into her dancing pole. She's carried off the stage; there's blood running from her nostrils.

A woman walks on with a donkey on a rope. It's wearing blinders with tiny sequins. The animal takes a leak against the stage light. It gives out steam and the woman waits with her arms crossed until someone mops the floor. She crawls under the donkey and moves her rear against his abdomen. Jesus, what is this? Then the lights go out. Drumroll, cymbal clash, spotlight on what the loudly braying donkey produces.

It's too late to avert my gaze. Victor is delirious with excitement, Jimmy sips at his glass, smirking. I reach my index finger all the way to the back of my throat while I fix my gaze on him. He looks back unaffected.

The breakfast hall is empty. I eat, but my stomach stays hollow.

It's stale outside, with smog everywhere.

In a sullen mood, I stroll around the shopping streets. In search of a present for Jimmy. Not because it's his birthday. Not out of friendship. Not to show respect. I wander through Hong Kong out of necessity: I want to pretend that nothing's the matter.

I come across Jimmy's Chinese sign, the rooster, in jade. A miniature as flat as the nail of my little finger.

The saleswoman shows me how to sew it into the lining of his jacket, so that it always brings good luck to him, invisible to others. She rattles on that only a gifted talisman brings fortune. Bought by the bearer it is worthless. I nod impatiently: yes, yes, I will personally unpick Jimmy's jacket. And thread the needle. Jimmy is superstitious. He will sit enraptured on a chair across from me, waiting for the good fortune that will never get away from him again. All thanks to me.

I don't get the chance to give it to him. Victor senses that I want to speak to Jimmy alone and doesn't let us out of his sight, not for a second. We're standing in the lobby. Jimmy wants to know some details about Holland's policy on compensations but Victor pulls him by his jacket toward the exit. I keep on top of my anger by deciding that I can give it to him later, my present.

I hurry along to the revolving door. There I mention the number of counter-orders that Holland has stipulated in America this year: Holland buys Joint Strike Fighters and Apaches from the U.S. but is allowed to produce the components in exchange. There's business in this for us. Jimmy shakes Victor off for a second. He asks if I have my report with me. Of course, it's in my room.

"Walk with me," I try.

"Walk with her," he says to Victor.

"Me? Why? We're in a hurry, Jimmy, we're already late," the little brat whimpers.

I leave them behind and take the elevator. I turn over my suitcase in a rush. No report. Impossible! I search everywhere. Gone.

When I return empty-handed to the lobby after fifteen minutes, it is deserted. The desk clerk tells me that Mr. Liu couldn't stay any longer.

"His taxi arrived."

His taxi? What? Where to? I call him up. His phone's off. So is Victor's. Shit.

Hope is no longer an option. Not as long as Victor exists. Three is one too many.

In my room I continue searching for the report. It's still missing. Fuck! I'm absolutely sure . . . Just as I'm cursing all and sundry, Jimmy calls. I ask where he is.

He says, "Yeah, sorry, Maria, we left in kind of a hurry. We had an appointment."

"Dammit, Jimmy! With whom, with what? A gambling den and a bottle of Maotai?"

"Victor and I have something to celebrate. You have to go to

Karachi. Yes, now. The cargo will arrive there tomorrow morning. Everything needs to be loaded into the terminal. Under your supervision. I'm counting on you."

It's three o'clock. He already booked a flight and a hotel for me. In two hours I have to leave. Details will follow by mail.

I want to say no. What do those two have to celebrate? I hate Karachi. Everyone is at war there. Before you know it, you walk into a firing line. You never know who's shooting at who but they're using live ammunition. It's just that I can't imagine what a refusal would bring about. I ask Jimmy when I'll get to speak to him again.

"Victor stays here and I'll catch up with you," he says.

"In a day."

Yeah, right.

The flight is a disaster. The plane swoops from one turbulence into the other and the man next to me fills up four sick bags. I get muscle soreness from all the times I've been leaning over discreetly into the aisle, as far away from him as possible.

I try reading the little guidebook: "In 326 before Christ, Alexander the Great sent his admiral, Nearchus, and the Macedonian fleet from southern Pakistan to the Euphrates. In the second century, Pliny the Younger and Ptolemy described four isles—Baba, Shampir, Keamari and Manora—that together formed a harbor. Starting in 1857, the British made the local fishing village Kalachi-jo-Goth into the port of Karachi on the Indus, point of departure for the annual pilgrimage to Mecca."

What the guidebook doesn't mention is that Karachi was once the greenest town of the subcontinent, and now is the filthiest. Three hundred thousand people used to live here; now we're up to twelve million, packed onto a slab of concrete. There is no place on earth where the difference between rich and poor is as pronounced.

After the independence of Pakistan in 1947, Karachi was overrun by millions of Muslim immigrants; the city became so overcrowded and corrupt that the government moved to Islamabad in 1960 and declared it the new capital.

Karachi's population continues to grow every year by 6 percent. There is a shortage of drinking water, electricity, sewers, houses, and roads. Of the thousand tons of garbage that are produced every day, only a quarter is collected. The place is swarming with rats.

It's a city of façades. Near the coastline we have tower blocks with a sea view, next are luxury apartments, followed by government rental homes, and then at long last the interminable slums where the people are so nauseatingly poor that no one can imagine that things will come together one day.

What isn't in the guidebook either is that Karachi sweats violence. Hate governs the relationships between ethnic groups, between religious groups, and between one and the other. Gangsters have divided the city in clearly delineated areas that are guarded by means of extortion and violence.

Because of the Afghan war, everyone has weapons. Heroin trade is everywhere, since the harbor of Karachi exports the opium that Pakistan cultivates, as well as part of the opium grown in Afghanistan.

This is my destination. This is where tomorrow a container ship arrives with a cargo that I have to keep watch over. We're talking carbines, tank parts, simulators, and RMP systems, Chinese versions of the FIM-92C, a portable Stinger. With that you can bring down anything flying at a height of up to twenty-five thousand feet, from your shoulder. Not exactly something to be handing out in Karachi. But it's a living.

I don't want to be here. Every taxi is dirty. Every taxi is full. Everyone here is crazy, the heat is unbearable, I feel sick.

An auto rickshaw drops me off at a dock area that stinks of rotting inland sea and dead stray dog. There's garbage in front of the hotel. I close my eyes, hoping that a Sheraton will rise up from the ground. Instead, an old codger with a fez walks out. He bows and smiles, repeats about ten times that his name is Nasir Irfan, he's a friend of Jimmy's. We climb three floors. Mr. Irfan carries my suitcase, I carry a bottle of water.

The room is tidy. The shutters closed. Mr. Irfan talks more than I can handle.

"Again: sorry about the elephant," he says. He shuts the door behind him. What? Elephant? Maria doesn't get it. Maria wants to sleep.

The rattling and clanking of chains outside wake me up. I push the shutters open. Downstairs torches are burning. Under my window lies a dead elephant. There are five people on top of it, carrying knives, and plates, and pans. They push and kick each other, argue over meat. The elephant is on its side. Trunk stretched. A blue tongue bulges out of its waggish mouth.

Elephants of the past used to be pitiful because they had to sit on little stools, or ride tiny bicycles. This elephant is having its flesh ripped off of its feet and buttocks.

I don't want to watch but do so anyway. The people on top of the elephant divide chores. One man cuts and hands out to the rest. The elephant becomes less whole, but no less elephant.

I'm still sitting there when everyone has long gone. Waiting for the day. And the flies.

I transfer myself to a Best Western Hotel. Mr. Irfan is wringing his hands while he explains to me that we're dealing with a circus elephant that accidentally got hit by a flying bullet during a parade, most deplorable, very coincidental, and unfortunately right next to his hotel. I nod. He asks if I have ever tried elephant curry before.

"Most delicious! For tonight the cook has . . ."

I shake my head, lift my suitcase off the bed, and leave.

The next morning I'm sitting in our Karachi office. Chief Inspector Kafeel of the harbor police called, it's urgent. Why? I thought everything was in order. *The Majestic* sails under a Pakistani flag. The captain is English. The cargo is covered by a hundred stamps.

Then Jimmy walks in with two officers. I hide my surprise.

"They were waiting for me at the airport. Something's wrong. We're leaving right away," he says.

With screaming sirens they drive us to the harbor. We don't exchange a word. Inspector Kafeel is waiting in the hall of the Karachi Port Trust building. Next to him are two police officials and three KPT gentlemen, all extremely nervous.

Fuck! What the hell is happening here?

Kafeel shakes hands in a hurry. As we're walking he tells us that our ship got stranded. Jimmy swears in Chinese. Kafeel explains that a deeply loaded vessel like *The Majestic* always has priority over all the other ships during high tide.

"Our pilot kept trying to make contact. But *The Majestic*

never answered. When the water went down, it became point-less. All of a sudden the ship set course for the harbor. It hit a reef, half a mile from the shore. Then the towing service tried hailing the ship. It took an hour to get a response."

Kafeel stands still and looks at us: "From an infant crying for its mother! We heard shots. Then we lost the signal."

Jesus. A child! Shots? The blood drains from Jimmy's face. Kafeel says, "The ship is surrounded. We're still hailing it. In vain. Mr. Liu, we need to be prepared for everything. You need to tell us all about the cargo, the ship, the owner, the crew. We need the waybill. You're transporting weapons and ammuni-tion. Can they be accessed?"

"The containers are sealed," Jimmy says unsteadily, "the crates themselves have been nailed down. The Stingers and the carbines can only be assembled by someone who knows what he's doing . . ." His voice dies down.

Everyone is quiet. Someone "who knows what he's doing" can blow up the harbor of Karachi with the snap of his finger.

There are ten people in the radio room. It's broiling hot and everyone bumps into each other. The harbormaster doesn't want to cause panic. Not a word gets out. As long as he doesn't know anything, he can't take action: clear the harbor, mobilize the marines, take control of the ship.

That child? What's it doing there?

Jimmy checks out names, I take care of the waybill and find us a plan of the cargo ship. We analyze every hold, every part of our shipment. We figure out who the crew is and where they come from. Fifteen members: fourteen Pakistani and one Eng-lishman, the captain.

Our buyer, the Pakistani military, is informed by Kafeel. *They are not amused.* There is cursing and swearing, that much is clear.

Five police boats are bobbing around the ship. We can't see them. Monotonously, someone is trying to make contact with *The Majestic.*

An hour passes. The radio room reeks of body odor. Jimmy calculates how much this joke is going to cost him. The ship owner is only insured for the cost price of the cargo. The transportation by trailer here in Pakistan, the stevedore, the rent for the terminal—everything has to be paid for. He yells into a phone that he refuses to do that and says curtly, "I missed the part where that's my problem!"

Just when I can tell by looking at him that he's thinking of entering the ship by swimming, Kafeel yells, "Sssst!"

From the speaker, the sound of a little boy calling for his mommy in English can be heard. The man operating the marine telephone asks the child for its name. No answer. Jimmy grabs hold of my upper arm and motions the man to make way. Goddammit, why me? Because I'm the only woman here?

"Hi," I stammer. "Hello? I'm Maria."

I hear the child breathe. Silence. What should I do? Jimmy makes an irritated gesture: *Go on!*

I don't know what to say.

The child sobs: "J.J. is hurt. His nose is torn."

I hope that J.J. is made of plush. I ask him. He says, "Hmmm," which sounds like a confirmation. When asked about his own name he answers, "Noah."

And then he says that J.J. is four already, and starts humming.

I sing some songs along with him. I make jokes. The men and Jimmy are sweating. The clock is ticking. Noah is uncontrollable, just like *The Majestic*. He plays with his teddy bear. Sometimes he talks to it. He tells J.J. not to meddle with the buttons again because "it makes Maria sad." Probably because I asked him to keep off the marine telephone.

We think he's the son of the captain, who appears to be called Noah as well. Besides, he tells us that he wore his daddy's cap today. We also know where he is. In the captain's quarters, his description of the view matches. Then he must be on the upper deck.

Time is running out. Soon it will be low tide. The ship could capsize, tear open, sink, explode, God knows what. The harbormaster ticks his watch in anger. He doesn't want scrap iron on the bottom of his shop floor, especially not when it contains tank parts and a few hundred Chinese versions of the FIM-92C. He hisses, "Have that kid find a grown-up!"

I cover the microphone and ask him if he's crazy. Shots have been fired. This is a matter of life and death! He says sardonically, "Life and death? *You sell weapons!*"

Jimmy interferes. He calms down the harbormaster and assures him I will find the right words. He nods at me. I take a deep breath and say, "Noah, you need to help me."

Two men had a fight. One of them had a gun. The other had a knife. Good, understood. What else?

"And then?" I ask.

"Then I went hiding."

"And your mommy, where is your mommy?" I ask.

"In England," he says, surprised.

Instantly Kafeel orders three officers to a side room. To track her down using the captain's address.

"Noah, do those two men know where you are?"

He tells me that he gets into the closet every time he hears something.

"Clever boy!"

He says, "The cook."

"What is the cook doing?"

"I don't think he's nice anymore. He threw daddy down."

"Where's your daddy now?"

"Here with me . . ."

Everyone freezes. I tell him to take his father's hand. Is it cold? Can he see his father's face? Is it very pale? Suddenly he starts to whimper in panic that he wants his mommy. He cries.

I swallow.

"Noah," I say, "we're going to play a little game: you can be the doctor, I will be the nurse, and your daddy is the patient. Okay?"

Okay. "Hello, Doctor, is our patient very cold? Is he very pale? Does he need any bandages?"

His father isn't cold or pale. He doesn't need bandages. There's no blood.

Thank God. I tell Noah that we're going to try and wake his daddy up.

The harbor police report that *The Majestic* shows a slight trim by the stern. Perhaps because of a leak. Or because the cargo has shifted. In two hours, the tide will be at its lowest point. Before that time the vessel must be set afloat. Kafeel confers with the harbormaster. Divers will be employed.

Noah gets to pinch his father's cheeks. Or his nose. Fun games. Together we shout in Daddy's ear that it's time for him to get up. My hands are sweaty.

Someone puts a note under my eyes: according to a neighbor in England, Noah is sailing with his father for the first time this summer vacation. Noah's mother is unknown to him: the captain is divorced.

The divers take to the water. The police report that the ship is tilting up more strongly. The divers approach *The Majestic* unseen, ready to enter, ready to attach tow lines.

A new sound. The captain comes to, throwing up. I think: *Got smacked, concussion.*

"Uh-oh! Daddy, you're sick!" I hear Noah say.

Everyone is dead silent. Then I try to talk with the captain.

Noah's father moans reluctantly, "Shiite cook with carbine against a Sunni boatsman. About Allah, about Muhammad, about a woman, about the shitty food on board."

"The crew?" I ask.

He's silent, thinking goes audibly slow, hurts: "Locked up. By the cook. Lower hold number four."

Jesus! Lower hold number four is full of tank parts. You're stuck: the ship heels over, two tons of steel slides straight at you. Behind you: the steel hull of the ship. Or worse: you're sinking and lower hold number four slowly fills up with water. Kafeel relays to his divers: twelve people in lower hold number four, carrying heavy load. Secure adult and child in captain's quarters, upper deck, starboard side.

Jimmy and I look at each other. His eye quivers at the thought of losing $40 million in goods. Genuine, honest goods.

Then everything takes a turn for the worse: paralyzed by

fear, we hear shots and harbor police screaming at the same time. Noah cries. I move the microphone away from me; it's impossible to gain control.

Later on, Kafeel recounts what exactly happened, using many gestures. The cook was running across the upper deck, the barrel of his carbine was jammed between the shoulders of the boatsman, who—hands behind his head—was forced to jump overboard. The shooters couldn't get a clear shot at the cook, it all went too fast and the distance was too great. They witnessed how the falling boatsman was being shot at in midair by the cook. And hit. Mortally, so it seemed.

This was the team's opportunity to move in and open fire on the cook.

We heard the salvos ricochet off the metal of *The Majestic* through the marine telephone. Ten divers entered the ship. The cook pulled the trigger in his mouth right before their eyes. We could hear their cries as well as the crack of the shot.

Then the divers got out the heavy guns and forced the latches. Of the twelve crew members two were heavily wounded, because they had been pushed down the ladder by the cook. Two containers had shifted because their tie-downs gave way. A part of the cargo had been exposed to seawater.

The reef had carved a three-foot rip into the hull.

I wait by the quayside for a rescue boat. *The Majestic* can't make the harbor during low tide. Jimmy argues with someone from the ship owner's company. Eventually, we learn not much damage has been done. I catch myself feeling relieved that most of the weapons can still be fired.

All of this transpired in just one bad morning. It seemed longer. Lunatics are everywhere: the Sunni boatsman complained about the meat and called the Shiite cook impotent. The rest of the crew—Sunni, for the most part—laughed at the cook, straight to his face, and shaped their hamburgers to look like drooping dicks.

I'm hoping to meet Noah and his father. Jimmy bought him the most expensive stuffed animal in Karachi, a rabbit. But the captain is in bad shape and Noah pretends he doesn't know me. He doesn't want the toy. He climbs into the ambulance with his dad.

Before I shake Kafeel's hand, we've become strangers to each other again.

That evening, Jimmy and I are dining by the seaside. Quiet at first, then talking at the same time. I tell Jimmy how disappointed Irfan was when I left his hotel. When I bring up the elephant curry and the obviously deranged cook, he roars out laughing, until I can see tears in the corner of his eye. I haven't heard him laugh like that for weeks. A burst of laughter in peaceful Karachi.

Life is good. Most of the cargo has been saved. I get to hang on to the stuffed rabbit. A cuddly toy for home. I could be the perfect mother.

Then Jimmy says, "I'm having a get-together. Two days from now. In Hong Kong. You should come."

When I arrive in Hong Kong two days later, I'm wearing Jimmy's houndstooth coat with his talisman in my pocket. There are many Chinese guests. I gently kiss Jimmy next to his eye patch. I'll give the present to him later. I decide to drink very little. The one who tries to force me into having a whiskey anyway is Victor.

"Thank you, Victor!" I would like to let the *r* roll until that idiot understands I'm making a fool of him.

He asks, "Has Jimmy told you already?"

Okay, I feel this one coming. He's going to announce something rotten with pleasure. Brothers Joe, Anthony, and Robert raise their glasses at me, in the distance. I blow exaggerated kisses at them.

He grins: "Have you found out why Jimmy and I had something to celebrate in Hong Kong? I got promoted. I'm the new managing director. From here on, I'm your boss!"

My smile petrifies, whiskey trickles down my chin, my trembling hand needs to put down the glass. He calmly hands me his card and says, "Managing director and business associate."

I'm furious. At him. At Jimmy.

"By the way," he says, grinning even bigger, "I found something. Rather careless, Maria."

Straight out of nowhere, he waves the lost report on Holland's compensation policy.

"Filthy rat!" I hiss. "You fucking stole that from my suitcase."

He just smiles: "That's not what Jimmy thinks."

He throws my report between the liquor bottles. Then he turns around and wants to leave. I hook my claws into his back panel and pull him next to me hard. I feel him paralyze with fear and bring my head up to his.

"Do you love him?" I hiss. I pull the cloth so tightly that it cracks. "Do you even care about him one bit, asshole?"

He doesn't answer. Of course not. I push him from me. He makes himself scarce.

* * *

I'm five glasses into the night, when Jimmy cheerfully comes walking toward me.

"What are you doing here out back, Maria, why don't you join us?"

He talks about Victor. That he'll be working for us. At the office. Great, isn't it? He'll do well. "Don't you think he'll do well?"

By now I've knocked back half a bottle of vodka, but my head is clear.

"What?" I lisp. "Victor? What is he good at? Weeeeell, what are whores good at?"

I say the verb. And again. I keep shouting dirtier varieties. I'm sweating. Where did all these spectators come from? Jesus, I'm just standing here striking up a good old conversation with Jimmy. I can see Joe's shocked expression. The other brothers have gone silent.

Just need to fix Jimmy's bow tie. It's a little crooked. He moves back, my hand floats in the air. Two steps and he's at the door. His eyes are still fixed on the floor. He holds the door open for me.

"Come on," I stutter, with indignation. "Just when we were having fun!"

I stay put, unstable, clutching my report. My head stings. Are we finished? But I still have a present. Why is everyone so quiet?

I look around amiably. The floor beneath my pumps starts wavering. I stumble past Jimmy, through the marble hall, into the bathroom, and empty my stomach. Then I press my quivering palms against my eyelids. The report is soiled. I wash it off but make it worse. I leave it behind.

When I get back, everything is as before. Jimmy's arm is still

holding the door open. I have to go past my boss and his speechless guests again to get my purse and coat, next to the stereo.
The bag dangles from Victor's fingers. He drops it right before
my nose.

"Oops," Victor whispers.

Picking it up requires effort. Patiently, Jimmy waits until I
walk out of his life. If he stays calm, it'll be quicker. I struggle to
my feet, wriggle into my coat, set course, and make myself flat,
not having to touch him. There's one more thing I need to say:
"The vodka here is watery and cheap." He turns away from my
breath.

Eleven steps before I reach the front door. It flies open and
then swiftly shuts again. I forgot my soft toy. The wind stirs the
blossoms. I stagger forth.

I'm right. Just very goddamn right.

CHAPTER 14

The DustBuster has lost its suction power. Now it just makes a lot of noise. Martin emptied the dust bag. It didn't help. Then he unscrewed it, blew into it, mumbled something, and put it back together. What's even handier than the handiest man in the world is a warranty and a receipt. It's not even a month old.

I'm outside, in front of the store, and see the salesman standing on one leg in the shop window. It's the same one from three weeks ago. His customer wants something that he can't reach in any other way. I think it's the red deep fryer, hope it is, because the pan is so far away that this prick has to try very hard to get it. If I open the door now, it would hit him in the head. He has it coming to him but I decide to wait.

I'm curious who the customer is that coaxed him into doing this. I bring my head up to the window and have a look inside. Shen-li?

"Shen-li!" I tap on the glass.

Shen-li looks up in surprise, recognizes me all of a sudden, and says a quick word to the salesman. He stiffly keeps his balance in the shop window. Shen-li opens the door to let me in. We both forget about the shopkeeper. I give Shen-li a kiss. He shouts that my cheek feels cold. We grin because of all the happy memories we share.

The salesman clears his throat. He asks Shen-li if he can be of any further assistance.

"No, I'll come back some other time." He looks at me: "And you?"

I look at the salesman. He almost sold a deep fryer. He failed because of me. Bad time to bring up a broken DustBuster.

I smile. "Me too."

"Moving," I say, pointing at the mess. My default apology for anyone who trips over the boxes.

"I kept saying that myself," says Shen-li. "Trust me, in the new house you'll still be doing it! It took me weeks to unpack everything."

I like his way of talking. You always feel understood.

He doesn't sit down, but leans against the counter. He's dark-haired, no gray ones yet.

Jimmy, I think. God, suddenly he looks like Jimmy.

"Something wrong?" he asks.

"Funny," I say, "you here."

We figure out how long it's been. He remembers when Nella was born. That was the last time. That's nine years ago. He's forty now. You wouldn't think by looking at him.

He rubs his hands: "What's keeping that coffee, Maria?"

I place a mug in front of him. We sit at the kitchen table.

I ask about his twin sister, Suze. He tells me she had twins herself.

"Two blond girls," he says, "with decent, good old Dutch names: Geerthe and Cathelijn." He smiles. "She lives in a village with her family now, no longer in the city.

"Blond girls," he says again. "Can you believe it?"

I kindly shake my head. And what about her job as head of the Mathematics Department. He says she tried but that she would rather stay with the kids.

"Doesn't it always go like that, Maria? Wasn't it the same with you?"

I nod, I smile. It doesn't matter what we're going to talk about: Jimmy's better half is here.

What's nine years? For Shen-li and me, nine years is nothing but a comma in a cheerful conversation that never seems to end. Perhaps that is why my questions are so few: I want to save some for later. Why talk about Jimmy now when we can still do that afterward? Hopefully, I'll keep running into Shen-li my entire life.

He tells me he was in a relationship. That his girlfriend ran out on him. That breakup, it still puzzles him, he says. "I was promoted. Got very busy. Too busy. Isn't it stupid that I was devastated about her leaving but didn't quit my job?"

He wants to know if I still have contact with the Liu family.

"At first I did, with Joe," I say. I stare at him. It's the first silence to occur. He nods. Why does he nod? Before he can say anything, I get up and ask if he wants some more coffee. Is he hungry? He looks at his watch. No, no, he's gotta run. But he had a great time. He gives me his cell phone number. I give him our new address. We promise to keep in touch. Not to wait until we run into each other again nine years from now.

He grips me tightly at the door and presses me against him. I open up, he steps into the doorway. The cold rises. I wrap my hands around my shoulders. He puts his scarf on.

Without looking at him I say, "I still appear to have a gun."

Perhaps he didn't hear me.

"Jesus!"

"It fell out of the linen closet."

"Jesus! What did Martin say?"

"I didn't tell him."

Now I have embarrassed him completely, and by panicking about it I'm making things worse. It just comes blurting out: "Do you still think about Jimmy a lot?"

I see him trying to imagine what it feels like: to think a lot about a father that you don't get to meet until you're eighteen and who powders the animal species that you're trying to protect in order to make impotence pills. Slowly he says, "Not very often. It had always been a difficult relationship." He sighs. "We tried."

I nod. I think about my old files and my gun turning up, about this encounter, and about the words "Hong Kong" and "Pakistan" that were casually dropped last week.

I slowly say, "I haven't thought about your father in a long time."

"That gun," he says, "what will you do with it?"

"What do you think?"

"You're asking me, Maria?"

He sees my confusion, takes a smiling step forward, and hugs me one more time. Then he heads down the walk. Yes, he looks like Jimmy more than he thinks.

He turns around and points his finger at me.

"We'll call!"

"Did you have company? Who was it? Was it fun?"

She lets her school bag slip from her shoulder and runs around the kitchen table. She spotted Shen-li's empty coffee mug. She hates it when she misses something. She climbs onto my lap and latches on to me. We're monkeys.

"An old friend."

"Best friend?"

"Mmm, maybe. Close."

"Something like me and Sjanna?"

I ask her in surprise if that is really true. She nods enthusiastically. I tell her that I like that. Much better than bullying each other. Right?

CHAPTER 15

I'm meeting Sulleyman in Chicago. He has a teak desk, a brunette serving coffee, and a view of Lake Michigan. He looks at me expectantly, arms crossed. What does he know? There's talk about the rift with Jimmy. Everywhere. Including here.

He says, "I don't balm wounds."

"No need to."

"Good. I can give you a job. And a lawyer to smooth things over. A good guy. I don't want a mud fight between you and Jimmy."

"I already have a lawyer. Since a month."

"Yes, that's what I mean," says Sulleyman.

He offers me a princely salary. I'm set up for life if I do this. I would like to start right away but he raises his hand.

"You'll run into him. Can you handle that?"

I tell him what he wants to hear.

He gives me a scrutinizing look: "And I deal in other things than Jimmy."

I laugh. I laugh straight to his face. Since yesterday, from now on, I'm selling *everything*.

After the party I went back to Jimmy's house. His servant sent me away.

The next day, in Holland, I went straight from Rotterdam Airport to the office. Victor stopped me. I refused to hand in my key, disappeared into my room, he stalked off, cursing. I turned my back to the door and called Jimmy. He was ranting and raving: "violation of authority to act," "cantonal judge," "nonactive," "resignation." These are the only words I can remember from the conversation.

The receiver got heavy, I started to breathe less and less deeply. Until I couldn't think anymore. I screamed back at him that I would file a goddamn complaint, that he was a rotten son of a bitch, that I would sue his ass. Jimmy yelled that we would let our lawyers battle it out. Shit! I smacked the telephone against the steel rack. The whole of the conversation took no longer than a minute.

Because I had no one else, Martin came over that night. I was glad he didn't say, "I told you so." He gave me the number of a lawyer. I didn't ask if he wanted to stay, if his new girlfriend knew where he was, but he didn't leave.

The lawyer asked if I had kept a record. I gave it to her. She leafed through it and said, "Your boss will have to pay considerably if he wants to get rid of you. Did you report for work yesterday? Have you discussed this matter with anyone else?"

Then she dictated a letter to her secretary I should use to file a complaint. The rattling of her keyboard sounded like a muffled Nazi MP 38.

Two days later, Sulleyman called. Was it time for a talk? Or was it still too soon?

The next day, I flew to Chicago.

Sulleyman works alone. He has accountants, secretaries, footmen, but no one for trading. Now he calls me into it.

Jimmy's terrified of Sulleyman. I'm not. I don't need to know who he is.

"Give me an assignment," I say. "One assignment, that's all I ask."

"You're moving to Chicago?" Martin asks.

"No. Not for now."

I don't ask if that makes him happy, because I don't want to think about his answer yet.

I learn a lot the next few weeks. About how freeze-dried microorganisms endure being used as heavy weaponry. About the technique for detecting aerosol particles that measure 0.8 by 4 microns and have a density of 1 gram per cubic centimeter: roughly the volume of an anthrax spore. And about micro-encapsulation: a "packaging method" to protect germs from heat, oxygen, light, and drying out. I read about microcapsules that, due to gas generation, open up in sunlight. Fired at night, they slumber, like their future victims, until just after the start of a new day.

I plunge headlong into my training over the next few weeks. My fingertips glide along the lines. I have to read them only once. Every time when Martin visits, I stuff everything under the couch.

I visit the firing range. I put in more hours of practice. Sulleyman wants to have implicit faith in me. The gun will be my
hand, my eye, my judgment. Arm stretched, I'll split mosqui-
toes, raindrops, sand grains.

I keep my body fit by kickboxing.

I make love to Martin in a way that must seem very strange
to him. I cut his baffled questions short. If he's scared, he should
get out. If he's interested in more, he can stay.

Shen-li calls, disconcerted with my resignation. I keep it
lighthearted. Let's get together sometime?

Mark the accountant calls: Now I can see for myself? Victor
is a whore and Jimmy is an asshole. I say, "I have to go."

Martin calls. No particular reason.

My lawyer calls. I won my case. Jimmy has to bleed. She
names the sum. I thank her. The telephone rings when I hang
up. I think she forgot something. It's Joe. It's the first time that I
speak to him since I got fired. I brace myself for a storm of accu-
sations, but instead he starts talking about nothing in particular,
and I listen till I've had enough and politely say I have to go.

Sulleyman is last to call: "Ready? No questions?"

He sends me off to Pakistan and Dubai. But first to a prelimi-
nary meeting in Rotterdam.

It's held in an empty school with tiled hallways. Jimmy and Victor also appear to be competing for the deal. Sulleyman didn't tell
me. I see Harry Chi, Renzo, the brothers Scholl, and the Pole,
Jakubowski. My appearance sets off a bout of thundering silence.

I take a seat, right in front of Jimmy.

Jakubowski icily concludes that Sulleyman is not yet
present.

"I'm negotiating in Sulleyman's name," I say calmly.

That dirty Pole is talking too loud, so I bring an end to that by slowly getting up and repeating myself—louder than before. Nobody says anything. Jakubowski mumbles something to Jimmy. I'm being frowned away by everyone. The Pole says formally, "You leave us no other choice than to postpone the meeting."

I look around the circle and get up again: "Fine. And brave."

The Pole already catches up to me in the hallway.

"It would have been different if Sulleyman had informed us of your attendance."

I turn around.

"It's your pick," I say. "Who do you want to go up against? Jimmy and Victor? Or Sulleyman and me? Against those two *has-beens* or against the big bucks? Go on, choose."

He stares at me blankly.

"Listen carefully, this is what you're going to do: you send Jimmy into the hallway for a minute. You make sure I can compete, and that Jimmy becomes the ass of the day for a bottom price. The computed compensation will be boosted, especially for Sulleyman and me. If not, then it's war."

The Pole shakes his head.

"Do it, man!"

He complies.

Within two minutes, Jimmy storms into the hallway, Victor stumbling in his tracks. Furiously he stands in front of me, flinging Chinese profanities in my face until he gets caught up in his own words, white with rage.

"You look pale," I say. "I hope you don't die."

I walk past him and step into the room again.

* * *

If I decide to take on Sulleyman's assignment, I'll be meeting someone called Umesh in Quetta, the capital of Balochistan. I'll hand him a disk in exchange for two Afghan boys. I'll receive a passport that lists them as my children. Umesh, acting as my husband, will travel with me to Dubai, because in the Emirates a brand-new future with wealthy parents awaits the boys.

"No, wait a minute, no smuggling job," I say decidedly. "Packages, children, what do you take me for? And why all the way to Quetta, the filthiest, farthest corner of Pakistan?"

Sulleyman explains that in Quetta, Afghan orphans are up for grabs. That this is a onetime job, that it happens to turn out like this, that I'm the right woman in the right place. He can't possibly pass for the mother of two kids, can he? There's a lot of money at stake.

I ask him what is on the disk, where he plans to have a gun ready for me, and who this guy Umesh is.

He seems slightly irritated, then he says, "The disk contains Israeli scientific research on the anthrax bacteria *Bacillus anthracis*. It's the report of a vaccination of 2,596 test subjects with a live anthrax vaccine. And Umesh has a gun. He'll protect you."

"No," I say, "I want my own gun. Traveling through Balochistan without a Glock? Jesus, man, how do you picture that?"

"You can move freely. The shalwar kameez you'll be wearing is recognizable for Umesh's people. They're everywhere."

"Invulnerable? Because of a dress? Do you think I'm going to a masked ball? I need more information."

He sighs. "Umesh is an alias for the former inspector general of Islamabad. A powerful man. He'll make sure that nothing happens to you."

My God! That's Chaudary, Jimmy's dirty friend! That son of a bitch with his stump dick at the police station in Islamabad. That sick bastard who forced his tongue down my ear.

I ask what Umesh looks like. Tall, glasses, a limp. Yep, Jimmy's pal.

Sulleyman doesn't notice anything.

Pondering, he says, "Maybe I was wrong. Maybe it's too much to ask. Maybe you would have gone along with it, had it been a job for Jimmy. You used to do everything for him. With love, I would almost add."

I only say, "Get me a gun."

He solemnly swears he will.

Quetta Airport, seven in the morning. Jimmy's friend is waiting for me. We recognize each other and don't say hello.

Chaudary watches, motionless, as I fetch my things from the baggage claim.

In an empty elevator we sink silently until we reach a concrete parking lot. As soon as I get next to him in the Mercedes, he locks the doors.

He smirks: "Together at last, Maria. Married, and well settled."

I grab the palm of his hand and let my tongue slip between his fingers. The grin freezes on his face. For a second there he wants to hit me, I can almost taste the blood on my lips. I act the injured innocent. He turns away from me and starts the engine.

My impertinence has scared him off. His respect for Sulleyman will do the rest. For now, at least.

"Little London," Quetta was once called, "refreshed by jasmine-scented breezes." Now the mornings are poisoned by exhaust fumes. The city lies, engirdled by mountains, at a height of fifty-five hundred feet. It's cooler up there than in the valley but also filthier and more dangerous.

Balochistan is the garbage dump where Allah dropped down the crap that he got stuck with after creation, according to the Pathans, and they know. They are familiar with the mountains and their nomads: both of them coarse and unpredictable.

I want to know where the kids are. Chaudary wants to see the disk. He won't get it until the kids have been delivered to their adoptive parents in Dubai and the money has been collected. He knows this. So we both shut up.

Hotel Quetta Serena gives us separate rooms with a door between them, its key on my side. I hear Chaudary draw a bath after prayer in the afternoon.

I put on a veil and slip out of the room. I hurry down the hall. Outside, I cross Hali Road and follow Zarghoon Road until I reach the entrance of Liaquat Park. I find Hotel Al Talib. I unhook the veil.

I ask the lady behind the counter about the present for Aunt Aleena. In a sincere voice she says that it cannot be exchanged. I answer that Aunt Aleena is crazy about chocolates. Then she hands me a package the size of a Glock.

"*Shukriya*," I say. "Thank you."

In the afternoon, Chaudary tells me what I already know: Tonight two children will be delivered, boys, two and four years old. Tomorrow evening we'll fly to Dubai, where we drop off the children at another hotel, with their future parents. Chaudary will collect a hundred and thirty thousand dollars there and take off twenty thousand for himself. The rest goes to Sulleyman.

I asked Sulleyman how well he knows Umesh.

"Umesh knows *me* well enough to know that he's got a problem if he doesn't do as I say. But why do you ask?"

"No reason."

"Relax. He knows who I am."

The little boys are lying in the bed, stunned. We get the rest of the tranquilizers for free. The oldest child is burning up. Fever. I tell Chaudary to get some fruit juice and an ice pack.

I roll the boy on his belly and turn up his shirt. Among the slashes and scars of innumerable assaults sit little red spots. Scarlet fever, measles, something like that. I take a look at his crown; hold my fingertips against his carotid artery. It's beating much too fast! If Jimmy were here, he'd say something stupid that would tell me what to do.

The ice pack doesn't help, the fever rises, and the boy doesn't drink. More spots keep popping up. They appear on his eyelids, inside his ear ducts, and by the end of the night even on the inside of his eyelids. He moans and I'm powerless. I want to get a doctor, but Chaudary will have none of it. The youngest child is constantly asleep and I don't know if that should worry me, but for now it is convenient. I'm exhausted.

Without giving me a hard time, Chaudary goes to his room. I keep the Glock on me, get in next to the oldest, who's burning like fire, and try to sleep. His name is Reza and he's in pretty bad shape.

I wake up early in the morning. Reza gasps for breath. I get dressed and grab the telephone. I ask the lobby to put me through to Shaleen Medical Complex.

Chaudary bangs on the dividing door, harder and harder. That prick! He'll wake up the entire hotel. I turn the key and take four quick steps back. I draw the Glock and point at his intestines, while my eyes force him back. Astonished, he lifts his hands. While I keep him covered, I scream into the telephone for an English doctor. Now. This instant! Without taking my eyes off Chaudary, I answer the questions of the pediatrician on duty.

"They're sending an ambulance," I say. "Up with those hands!"

"You're crazy! We have to get out of here. If he dies, they'll check out who we are!"

Behind my back Reza's lungs are wheezing for oxygen. The youngest, Najim, sleeps through it all.

"Then I suggest you get down on bare knees and pray to Allah for his recovery."

He curses and spits at me but doesn't dare move. He doesn't calm down until I tell him that a dead child will cost us money, a lot of money.

When there's knocking at the door, I put away the gun. Two male nurses kneel by the bed. They open Reza's eyelid, feel his wrist, and put him on a stretcher. They shout something at Chaudary that I don't understand. I wrap the sleeping youngest boy in a towel, pick up my passport and veil, and follow the stretcher.

"You stay here," Chaudary snaps at me when we are standing outside. He pushes me away from the ambulance and climbs in himself. My dress and the weight of the youngest boy prevent me from reacting quickly. The last thing I see: Reza under an oxygen mask. The car takes off with screeching tires.

* * *

After an hour he calls me. Reza is dead. I need to listen carefully. Very carefully. I need to go to the airport and leave for Dubai today, with Najim. Now, tonight. He says the name of the hotel. He says the name of the couple who will pick the children— child—up. I need to keep the disk close to my body and get rid of the Glock.

While he continues talking about what I have to do, I get a second call. In a reflex I put Chaudary on hold. It's Jimmy. Jesus! He wants to know who he's talking to.

"Me," I say, confused.

He swears and cuts me off. I switch back to Chaudary. He hung up. The child in my arms is starting to wake up. It cries.

"Umesh will take care of himself," says Sulleyman. "I'm sure he'll get to Dubai in time."

"But that little boy, Reza . . ."

"Yes, a terrible shame. Just divide the asking price by two. That will be the new amount. I think I'll just pay Umesh his part. Better luck next time."

Because I'm very silent, he says, "The boy wouldn't have lived much longer, there where he came from. Every extra day was a blessing."

We're in Dubai. It's late in the afternoon. Chaudary informs the adoptive parents that Reza's dead. They barely react. Perhaps I just don't get Arabs and their emotions. Perhaps the shock doesn't get through to them. Perhaps Najim, who's running around the hotel room holding his drinking cup, is reason enough to be happy. But they're definitely not sad.

Chaudary counts the money. We shake hands. The man picks up Najim, who starts to shriek. He reaches out his fingers at me and screams when he's carried out of the room and into the hallway, until his voice reverberates inside my head alone.

I didn't say hello to Chaudary when we met and won't be waving him off now. That he saved me from a police hearing by pushing me away from the ambulance doesn't change the fact that he's the bastard who once tried to abuse me.

He gives me Sulleyman's part of the money and I hand him the disk. Our only topic of conversation was Jimmy, and that is completely worn out. We take separate taxis to the airport and after the first bend I lose sight of his.

What the hell do I tell Martin? "Yesterday I had to smuggle a couple of kids into Dubai, one of them died on me! Called in the doctor a little too late . . . what have you been up to?"

I have an appointment with Shen-li. We go bar-hopping in Utrecht. With a friend of his, Peter. He works for UNICEF. A regular nice guy. When you hang around regular people too much, you get a conscience.

We have a drink, the place has a nice buzz. When Shen-li starts talking about Jimmy, I shrug. The music is loud, so I can't exactly hear what he's saying. He goes to get beer.

I ask Peter what it is that he does at UNICEF. At first I pretend to be listening. Then I hear him say something that forces me to look at him, whether I want to or not. He tells me a thing I had been wondering about but definitely didn't want to know. What he says had been lying in wait somewhere deep inside me and is now causing a splitting headache.

Shen-li returns with the beer. I say, "I'll be right back."

The boys nod and begin talking.

I find the exit just in time and lean against the wall outside, limbs trembling. I have to focus really hard when searching for Martin's number. *Pick up, please pick up.* My body feels as if it took a beating. *Pick up the damn phone!*

"Martin."

"Help me," I cry.

"And so?" asks Sulleyman.

"So this is where it ends, Sulleyman. I quit. You knew all about it. Those children are being abused as camel jockeys by a bunch of goddamn towelheads. A skanky million-dollar industry. And you're taking part in it. Little boys, three or four years old, taped down to a camel for hours and hours! By the time they're six or seven, they raise millions of dollars racing. For you. They don't get anything to eat, because weighing more than fifty pounds makes them worthless. Whoever falls and breaks something is shot. You knew exactly what was in store for Reza and Najim and yet you lied. You pretended that they would be well off."

He looks at me, fiddles with his pen. "Did Jimmy never lie to you?"

"Never," I lie.

"And you also left him."

"Yes? So?"

"Perhaps because he saw that you were unfit for this line of work. If that is true, it will be pretty difficult to learn to live with yourself. You'll be asking yourself how to explain this to your children. Things like that . . ."

I smile politely. "Nice try."

He returns a polite smile. "Anyway, thanks, on behalf of me

and that bunch of goddamn towelheads. Najim will bring in more than he cost me."

Martin's proud of me. Now that I've quit my job for good, he doesn't want to rent a house any longer. He's going to find us a house for sale. I erase the business numbers from my cell phone's memory. It's like washing sand from my eyes, unbuttoning something that fits too tight.

I erase all numbers. I only hesitate at Jimmy's.

CHAPTER 16

The front door is wide open. All the heat escapes. Nella and Sjanna are constantly running in and out, screaming with laughter, until I shout, "Hey, hey, hey!" and slam the door in their faces. When I slowly open up again, Nella makes a quarter of a turn so that she's standing with her back to Sjanna, who fishes a snow-covered envelope out of Nella's hood. She salutes.

"The apple pie recipe from my dad."

"How nice, Sjanna!"

Mirjam said to me on the phone, "Everyone thinks it's delicious. And it's not hard to make."

Those telephone conversations are becoming ever so pleasant. I must have sounded very enthusiastic about the apple pie, probably because Mirjam is so nice. I should have known that she would send the recipe along shortly after. Mirjam is a quick believer.

The pie is baked upside down. The slices of apple go on the bottom of the baking tin, on top of a layer of butter with sugar. First you caramelize the apple slices on the stove. Let them cool off.

Then you cover the baking tin with shortbread. Mirjam under-lined these words. You need flour, cold butter, sugar, eggs, and salt. Knead it, wrap it up in plastic, and put it in the fridge for an hour.

I take another glance at the note. The kids have gone upstairs already. Their wet rubber boots are lying around in the hall. I've stopped complaining. I'll wait until we're in the new house.

Pie. Whenever someone else bakes it, I eat pie. Sjanna has her father for that. Martin thinks he doesn't belong in the kitchen. I'd love to get him there just once. If I ever see Sjanna's father, I'll ask him how to get my husband to slap on an apron.

"He sometimes braids my hair. He's very quick at that, I never have to sit still for long," says Sjanna. "It's too bad he's in Hong Kong all the time."

She can join the circus any day; the corners of her mouth point up too much. She's sweet. Hard to imagine her getting bullied.

Sjanna rolls a cheese slice around her fork. I see how Nella squeezes all sorts of cold cuts between two slices of bread, together with cheese, lettuce, and tomato. The only one who thought this to be normal was Jimmy.

I notice that Nella is starting to resemble him more and more. Not Martin or me, but Jimmy Liu. As if I had been subject to his awkward manners during pregnancy to such an extent that they were passed on to the fetus. Especially these last few weeks have been revealing. It makes me think of Jimmy more than I would like to.

Nella asks if she and Sjanna can draw and paste at the kitchen table. I say yes. And that I like it when they do that. They want me to join in.

"Sure," I say.

* * *

Three nights ago I was walking with Toby, through the snow, to the canal. I always walk the dog right after dinner. Martin puts everything in the dishwasher and Nella watches TV, after she pretends to help clear the table. I saw them when I walked past the window. As if looking at my family inside a shoe box. Toby didn't like the snow that night. He had me pull the leash.

By the canal we slipped down the slope. There's no bridge out there. The dog was scared, but I didn't dare unhook his leash. He would run back up and stand there yelping. It would attract people.

I felt inside the pocket of my coat and put my fingers around the ice-cold Glock, ready for the pitch. There wouldn't be a splash. The noise of the freeway was too loud for that. I tried to look over my shoulder. I was alone, I've had plenty of occasions. I got cold. And the dog was whining the whole time. I couldn't do it. I turned around and started groping up again.

At the garden fence I waited awhile. Then I turned, ran the whole way back to the canal without falling, slid down the slope, and hurled the Glock away from me. The dog was at a complete loss and wanted to jump after it, straight into the deadly black water. I could barely grab him by the scruff of the neck. I dropped down in the snow, panting, him in my arms, no gun.

How does it feel, no gun, how does it feel? my thoughts raced. Except for the snow and the hard cobblestones, it felt good— naked, but good.

"What should we paste?" I ask Nella.

We have Magic Markers, beads, glitter glue, and colored paper.

There are brushes, scissors, and paint. We're going to make invitations for a party they'll supposedly be throwing soon.

"Not a real one," says Sjanna.

"No, we're playing sisters that pretend," says Nella.

"Yes. Sisters with the same birthdays."

"So they give a party together."

It's light inside because of the snow, all our things lie colorful around us.

I right myself. I hum. I put a saucepan on the stove and open up the fridge. I take out the milk. I pour some milk into the saucepan and turn on the gas. I stir a blend of cocoa, sugar, and water in the pitcher. I use the back of the spoon to crush the sugar lumps. I pour boiling milk through a little sieve and onto the mixture, tap the sieve, stir one more time, and divide the chocolate milk into three cups.

All in all, we cut and paste twenty invitations.

"Plus two spare ones," Nella says.

We calculate how much pie we'll need. Sjanna thinks we can cut eight wedges from the apple pie.

We stop to consider paper chains. Are they too old for paper chains?

Nella says they are. Sjanna says they're not. They look at me. They want something else to do.

"What are you going to get each other?" I ask.

A smart move. They divide the playthings and sit back to back, playing and giggling.

I get up to start dinner. I put the three used cups in the dishwasher. Take the potato bucket out of the sink cabinet and the curly kale out of the fridge. I look for a peeler in the drawer. I carefully rummage around in the compartments until I find it.

"We won't give each other the presents until it's really our birthday," says Nella.

I say I think that's a good idea.

Five o'clock. They switch on the light themselves. I tell them that I'm taking Toby for a walk. I ask them to put everything away in the meantime.

"Sjanna, is someone coming to pick you up, or do I have to drive you?"

She says her father is coming to get her at half past six. He's in town for the rest of the week.

"How nice, that means I'll get to see him," I say.

I call Toby and attach the leash.

With the knob of the front door in my hand I hear Martin's car door slam shut. I let him in and give the dog just enough leash to jump up against him.

"How was your day?" he asks.

"Nice. I had a nice day," I say. "A really, really nice day."

The dog park is just around the corner. I follow Toby. He's off-leash. He listens when I call him. I always run into the same people, with the same dogs. We have the same chats as always. Toby does his thing. The snow becomes a yellow slush underneath his lifted paw. We can go back now. I put the leash on again.

Among the houses there's a smell of baked onions and sauerkraut. Stomach hungry, ears cold.

The metallic beige BMW in the driveway must belong to Sjanna's dad, the apple pie dad.

I turn the key, smiling, push the front door open, and unleash the dog. I hear Martin talk.

Cheerfully I step into the warm living room. A somewhat chubby man turns around. Together with Sjanna. She comes up to his chest. She radiates joy.

"I want you to meet my dad," she says.

I don't blame Martin, looking back. He couldn't possibly have known who he'd let into the house. Never before had he met the man who, nowadays, appears to be with Sjanna.

The chubby man and I never blink our eyes, our mouths give nothing away. We shake each other's hand as if we don't fall through the scenery together, as if no before exists and no coincidence either. It looks as if we've been rehearsing this for years in front of mirrors and rolling cameras.

"Hello, Maria," the chubby man says firmly.

"Hi, Victor," I say.

CHAPTER 17

I haven't left Sulleyman a day before Joe calls. It's always Joe who calls. Even right after the rift between Jimmy and me, he continued to stay in touch. We never discuss what went wrong. We talk about cookbooks, about the kids, and about nonsense. He tells me something about Terrence, Jimmy's old Scottish terrier.

He says, "Jimmy loved animals."

"Yes," I say, "after all, he liked to treat me like an animal as well."

My sharp tone is meant for Jimmy.

We fall silent. Funny, why did Joe say "Jimmy *loved*" instead of "Jimmy loves"?

I ask him how Jimmy's doing and gather right away: not good.

"He's seriously ill, Maria."

Perhaps you start doing crazy things as soon as you find out that you're seriously ill. You destroy your company. You fire everyone, waste all the money. It's easiest to rob a business when you have no conscience and an expensive boyfriend. Of course, you tell no one a thing about your illness. That's how Jimmy did it.

He's lost weight. But not dramatically. It makes his neck look longer, his movements smoother. His skin gleams, he's been lying in the sun. He extends his hand. It enables me to feel how far it has progressed, he can't muster up a firm handshake; the fingers have started to feel brittle; squeeze harder and something breaks.

This is his villa, southwest of Hong Kong, on a hill. Idyllic, not a trace of death in the blossoms of the cherry trees. He's wearing a black silk turtleneck on top of his branded jeans. He serves tea in Wedgwood. His shoulder blades are dimly outlined through the fabric.

He tells me that his children came to visit. "It was nice," he says, "but they kept bringing up their mother. To be honest, I had hoped that they would have more of my traits. Their mother should have just told me about the pregnancy back then, so I could have been their father from the start. What can I do now? I've always wanted children but just didn't realize it. Everyone wants children, right? Don't you want to have children, Maria, someday?"

I ask about Victor, as casually as possible, because he disappeared on the first day of chemotherapy. Joe told me.

"Heard little of him since."

He says it without bitterness. I think: *He'll turn up again as soon as there's something to be divided.*

All of this comes too late. There's nothing to clear up or talk over. I was furious. Can only picture him as someone who did damage to me. He lights a cigarillo. Sure, why the hell not?

Can I do something for him? He looks past me as he blows out smoke, hopes to avoid an instant no that way. He's got a problem that I alone can help him with. He starts a lengthy explanation I can summarize in just one sentence. He doesn't have anything to shoot with anymore.

"Nothing? I'm sure you've got plenty," I say, trying to buy some time. Nerves make my voice go up. He shakes his head. A little sad. Shit. Jimmy doesn't have his Arminius anymore, his Walther, his Tanfoglio.

"Well," he says with a thin smile. "It happened while I was in hospital. Robert and Joe kept looking until they found everything: the cartridges, my permits . . ."

Just in case I had the idea that I was here because he missed me or because cancer changes you . . . he just wants me to get him something. Nothing's changed.

"And what about your business buddies, like the Triad boys in Beijing? Can't they fix you up?" I sound more irritated than I want to.

He smiles: "They don't grant me a quick death, Maria."

We're both silent. I know what's coming up.

He says, smiling, "Your gun, and then: poof! The Hemingway method."

He gives me an expectant look. Words occur to me that, if I try my best, will sound ridiculous enough to break the tension: apartment building, jump off (somersault); wrists, razor (avoid Hong Kong pocketknife); wrong lane, driving (in Victor's Lotus). But they're useless to him. For him there's only one way. No one understands that better than I do.

What is he doing, standing with that teapot in his hands?

Look at him, he doesn't shake, looks good. It's all still so far off. I tell him that.

He says, "Yes," puts the teapot down, and starts talking about the flagstones of his terrace, how difficult it is to lay them properly on forest soil. After thirty minutes he gets tired. I get up, he shakes my hand.

"Come again, Maria."

I promise without looking at him.

Utrecht is far away from Jimmy. Out here, you fill your life with things. Real things. There is no time for thoughts.

Martin and I visit a Realtor. I find a job working as a secretary at a law firm and take the neighbor's cat to the vet. The neighbors are on vacation and the animals I have to look after always get sick or run away.

"He doesn't want to eat."

"Haven't you felt the lump by her tail?"

"It's not my cat."

"But if you were to stroke her, just like this, on her back, then you would clearly feel a swelling here."

He looks at me as if I come from an island full of animal abusers, drinking blood-red cocktails under plastic palm trees. He's almost right and I don't mind.

There are more lumps to be felt.

"A matter of three or four weeks. She'll get pain. Bring her here then, we'll put her to sleep."

He carefully slips the cat in the basket and closes the little door.

* * *

I want to go to Hong Kong, I *have* to go to Hong Kong. I can't. I'm stuck with a sick cat until the neighbors get back. One more week. Use that week. Think, Maria. How do you get Jimmy a gun? There's no way my Glock will make it past the border, no delivery service or customs officer will fall for that.

I try to force myself to come up with a solution. Nothing presents itself. Shit, wait! The Sphinx! There's still a Sphinx sitting in a safe-deposit box in Islamabad. That gun I had a little adventure with down at the Margalla Hills when I was waiting for Jimmy's friend. I still have the key.

Is Jimmy fit to travel? Jimmy would have to pick the gun up himself in Islamabad. And then stay there. And use the gun there. Swiss craftsmanship, that Sphinx, nothing wrong with it, always works. "The Hemingway method" with a lifelong warranty.

But if he insists on dying in Hong Kong, we have yet another problem on our hands. The only way for him to enter China unnoticed is through the Khunjerab Pass. That journey would be too rough on him, he'd never survive!

I laugh out loud at this thought. Making sure Jimmy stays alive so he can put a bullet through his head, from a gun that was smuggled out of a country where you can get yourself shot in the neck for that. Timing is everything.

There was a time when we wouldn't shy from a transport over the Khunjerab Pass. Crates full of Kalashnikovs, FIM-92 Stingers, and other dangerous toys went across the border without a hitch thanks to our power, our influence, our bribe money, Jimmy's standing, and my reputation. Now it's all down to one wretched little godforsaken peashooter that would end up on the desk of one miserable, drab civil servant when the day is done. And that popgun is going nowhere. Because Jimmy's now a king without a land and I'm a simple civilian.

Is there really no one from Hong Kong's night circuit who is willing to sell Jimmy a gun? No. Not if the big bosses won't have it. In that case he couldn't even get a toenail clipper. Fuck! I have to go myself, it's the only solution. I have to get hold of a gun and bring it to Jimmy. But I don't want to be linked to his death. No one can even assume that I'll be meeting with him there. Even if he fires the shot himself his family will still see me as the killer.

I'll miss Joe. He's been more of a friend than Jimmy ever has. Joe's the man you need, but Jimmy's who you pick in the end. It's always been like that.

I dial Jimmy's number in Hong Kong but put the phone down immediately. It's nighttime over there. I have to go to sleep. The cat hoists itself onto the bed and tucks away her stiff paws very slowly.

In the middle of the night the cat wants to go out. After that I lie awake. Morning in Hong Kong. I put on a sweater and a pair of warm socks and crawl into a corner of the couch with the phone. It rings at Jimmy's end. Eight times. Ten times. No one picks up. The ringing stops. I check the number. Dial it again. It's eight-thirty over there. Jimmy always drinks coffee at eight-thirty sharp. Always. Shit, now what? Should I call Joe?

He picks up right away. He sounds worried.

"What do you mean, 'Jimmy's gone'?" I ask.

"He seems to be gone. He didn't show up for treatment at the clinic."

I try to reassure us: "Don't panic, you know how he is. Jimmy used to disappear all the time. No use asking questions about it afterwards. He's probably well enough to get out of it for a while. He's just living it up. That's a good thing, right?"

We chat some more, hang up. I'm not worried. Not one bit worried. A good way to get rid of that trip to Hong Kong. Right. Back to not caring.

The neighbors think their cat has gotten really skinny. I explain it to them. I hope they understand. He accepts the unopened tins, she picks up the cat with care. He props my door open with his elbow. Not saying a word.

I'm an invaluable secretary. My boss is a dick with a pin-striped suit and campy designer glasses. One morning there's a vase of tulips sitting in the way on my desk. He says it's secretary day. He asks how my former boss let me know that he was satisfied.

I deliberately answer, "He gave me a Sphinx."

He moves his chin like, "Oh," as if he knows what it is.

He only knows the word "Sphinx" in connection to "pyramids" and vacation plans that never came through.

I'm standing in front of my bedroom window, it's dark and late. I'm never tired anymore. A torch is burning in the neighbors' garden. The man from next door is digging a hole a little bigger than a cat. He's cutting layers of clay and stacking them neatly next to the hole. My eyes search for something wrapped in a blanket or a shoe box with a tail tip sticking out. I stop to consider pets. Maybe I'll have a bird someday. Or a piranha.

I think I'm putting it together nicely at that law firm. So does Martin.

"Nice!" is what he says, when I tell him that I've never felt so peaceful.

"Great!" when I start talking about a cockatiel. "Or do you want to start working on a baby?"

Jesus, what should I say? My hormones are acting all weird, I'm getting a lot of headaches. It starts in the morning when I get up and goes on until I fall asleep. Not every day but more often than before.

I've stopped calling Joe. Not that I'm unwilling to call. It's just the time difference, I guess.

I would have liked to get an answer to the question that I stopped asking myself a long time ago. That question finds its way to my brain at times when a bad song or a TV series full of broken-down love makes me cry. Why the hell was I never invited to Jimmy's funeral or cremation?

I can't convince myself that he's still alive. It's been eight months since I was with him, on his hill.

Eight months ago that I refused to help him. After that he went away for a short while, came back, and probably told his family, "There's one thing that I know for sure now: I don't want Maria present."

Was that how it went? I picture myself a long death struggle, full of visions about the time and pain the gun of a friend could have saved him . . . No, if I'd been Jimmy, I wouldn't have invited me to the funeral service, not under any circumstances.

Together with Martin, I'm moving to a house in a suburb. No more bars or smart shops around the corner, but a children's farm. When I ride my bike to work in the dark mornings, I can follow a cartoon series for five miles on end over the heads of children, some still in their pajamas, others ready for school, living room after living room, the TV set always in the same place stuck on the same channel.

When Joe calls, his voice is clear. So very clear. He apologizes, so do I, it's a custom. We talk fast, at the same time, we have to get through this. What he wants to say, I guess, is this: Jimmy passed away.

That's what he's calling about? They actually don't know. Still no sign of him. The family has been searching for months.

I curse to catch my racing breath.

"Come to Ontario, Maria, and help us."

"Didn't he leave a note or something?" I ask. "For your mother, for Victor?"

"No, nothing."

"Has Anthony traced his credit card through his bank yet?"

"Yes, Jimmy took out all that was left in one time. An estimated one million dollars, via Luxembourg and Beijing."

Shit, gambling money. Kept "untouched" outside of the business. Maybe he needed my gun for totally different matters? I don't tell Joe anything. I promise to call him back tomorrow.

I take some time off. Martin asks when I'll be going. In two days. "For the last time," I say, "probably."

Did he really think it would be over? He shakes his head and asks, "Are you doing this out of guilt or because you want to find him?"

What does it matter?

"Never mind," he softly says, and presses me against him. I'm surprised. He means it.

* * *

Scarborough, Toronto, Jimmy's father and mother. The brothers have tried to find Jimmy. His credit cards are gone, his passport. Through the pharmacy they found out that he ran out of pain-killers two months ago.

There's ten million in debts. No one knows who's gonna pay for them. Anthony estimates that Jimmy's got a million dollars in his pocket, all dirty. It's useless to approach morgues or hos-pitals if you don't know where to start. The police won't use the word, but today he's gone missing for exactly six months. Miss-ing: as if you can say that about someone who doesn't want to be found. It seems safe to assume that *Jimmy has left the building*. With enough money to be invisible. And to buy himself a thou-sand guns.

I understand why they kept me out of it for such a long time. I know how it goes in Chinese culture. Always solve your prob-lems within the family. They must be desperate. I'm the only one who knows the way to the shadowy underworld where Jimmy is hiding. If he's still alive. If, if, if.

His brothers don't want to know why he did it. I have to col-lect and deliver him. That's all. They're ashamed. For having to bother me with this. So they make sure that I end up at the lake with Joe by the end of the day. It's his honor to beg me into stir-ring up a hornet's nest. Do I want to go to Beijing: approach Sung Mah and the bosses of the Triad?

I'll do that.

Joe says, "We thought we'd made a smart move by taking all his weapons. Who would think of running away? He could have found rest here, no?"

I nod.

* * *

In the plane to Beijing I make a list of questions. It's hard. I try to come up with a schedule. Who do I approach first? What's the best way to go underground?

A day later, everything changes. I've come to meet Sung Mah. He knew everything. Controlled everything. I was afraid of him. Now he appears to be dead.

His assistant at Planeco told me, at a Formica table with an edge that looked eaten into, in a canteen smelling of tea. The boy sketched the outlines in melodious English. Seven months ago Sung Mah was shot in front of his apartment. The culprit escaped.

Then the assistant leaned forward, whispering, and told me everything in a single rush of words. How many bullets had shredded Sung's scrotum to pieces. How Sung had lain there, squirming. That it wasn't an ordinary murder but a message. Ten bullets through a scrotum is overdoing it if you just want the person dead.

In the end, he smiled: "But what exactly did you want to ask him?"

I told him that it no longer mattered. I'm walking aimlessly through Beijing now.

In the evening I call Martin. He asks me how things are going and I say, "Great."

I wake up early. Quan Je De, the restaurant where the boys of the Triad meet, is not an option until nighttime. Earlier is pointless, there's no one during the day. I go out for a walk.

I avoid the markets and their fetid, half-dead merchandise, zigzag through the crowd, and find a shop that sells enameled chopsticks. When I'm outside again, I see Jimmy. Shit, goddammit, it's him! He's walking on the other side of the street, fast, on his way to something. I don't shout, don't whistle through my fingers. Between us: three lanes of cars, bikes, the sun, sitting low, blinding me in spots where buildings are lacking. I run parallel to him, am unable to cross. He stoops down. It's not him. Oh God, it's not him.

Wheezing and sweating, I return to the hotel.

Quan Je De is crawling with Americans and Frenchmen. They're drunk and act obnoxious. The tourist traps are short of hands. Across from me a fatso's dipping dumplings in his beer. The dough becomes soft and sinks to the bottom of his glass.

I've been sitting here for an hour. I walk over to the side and ask the bartender in my best Chinese where I can find Wo Sun Yee. I point at the curtain. I know that's where the secret door is. He looks at me with a dumb expression. I must have pronounced it badly, there's simply no way of making myself heard through all the noise.

I fetch a beer coaster and write down the names of the three Tai Los that I'm looking for: Lee Mon, Shing Kwan, and Wo Sun Yee. I also include my own name. And that of my hotel.

The bartender accepts the coaster. He goes into the back, returns with a Chinese in an apron. Before I know it, they grab hold of me and throw me out.

The door locks behind me.

Beijing without Jimmy is good for your night's rest. It's the first time that I've gone to bed this early and bored.

At two o'clock someone knocks on my door. My hand glides along the wallpaper, looking for the light switch. Wearing nothing, I pick a garment off the floor, think about my bad breath, my sleepy head. Thank God the door is locked. Chinese people walk straight into your room. I set the door ajar. A boy, a letter. Yes, great, fantastic. I close the door again, fumble around for some change, in a front pocket, open the door again. We make the trade. I push the door shut with a bang. Idiots.

Wo Sun Yee has invited me for the following afternoon. To a public garden near the stadium.

I'm at the tearoom at the designated time. Wo Sun Yee is already there. He slopes forward slightly, something between nodding and bowing. This is the first time that we have met each other. I sense that there are bodyguards strolling around the parlor. We don't see them but they won't look like nice guys.

"Jimmy?" he asks.

I nod. "Jimmy."

It feels as if I'm enjoying the lovely weather with my grandpa. He's open, explains what Jimmy came for.

"He wanted a gun. I can't say that he looked dying to me. He had to take care of something. And he spoke of his children, wanted to arrange something for them, having to do with money. I didn't inquire any further."

"Jimmy feared that you wouldn't grant him a quick death," I say.

He nods and says:

"Ours is a strange line of business. We sell thousands, tens of thousands of guns, with ease. We never ask who will use them and why. And then this one man, who's as good as dead, who no one wants to soil his hands on. I gave him my own gun."

Wo Sun Yee did what I should have done. Dammit.

"Do you really need to find him, Miss Staal? I promised him peace for the time he has left. We gave him a new identity."

He puts Jimmy's old passport and his credit cards in between us on the table.

"You see, his grandfather was a good friend of mine. Jimmy greatly resembles the man. They won't let anything stop them, go straight through walls. If Jimmy did have one more task to complete, he won't die until it has been completed. And if he has succeeded by now, he is dead."

He brings his face close to mine.

"Miss Staal, what can you do for Jimmy if he's still alive? What can you offer him? You are more limited in your freedom than he is. His body makes it hard on him but you are hostage to your own concerns, your longing for the past, and your guilt. He doesn't want to be found. Allow him that."

He takes two taffies from the pocket of his jacket. He offers me one. It's very sweet. He takes the other. We sit like this for a while. He gets up, makes his bow, and says goodbye.

I disgust myself. No one sees that I'm lying. I tell everyone in Scarborough that Jimmy passed away. His mother cries. Dammit!

I say that I've found out, thanks to the Triad bosses, that he died from a bullet to the head fired by himself, in Pakistan. And that he was cremated at the Karachi morgue, after the standard period of preservation, since no one came to claim his body. A version that perhaps isn't really watertight. But more importantly, it's coming from Maria. So to them it's true. Jimmy's dead.

I give Jimmy's things to Joe, who is too sad to ask further questions.

* * *

A memorial service is held in a Canadian church and I'm attending it. I'm leaning against Martin because I have the flu that day. My body breaks in half with every step I take. I don't hear, see, or understand much of all that's being said or done.

Shen-li and Suze are present, some old colleagues, and a single unknown business buddy. Not Victor. There are other people, many people, entirely unknown to me, people Jimmy never told me anything about, and flowers, including ours. I have to get to bed, it's so cold.

Searching stops when you run out of money. When you're tired. When you've been everywhere and no one helps you anymore. When family and friends tell you—first smiling, then threatening—that they will lock you up or abandon you. When someone doesn't want to be found.

In your head the searching never stops. No memorial service is equal to the conviction that someone is still there. You can hold a funeral oration, listen to sad music, and cry until you're blue in the face. You can burn an empty coffin, offer your condolences, act as if your life goes on, but when you keep believing that somewhere on this earth there's a person hiding away, who is better off than you are with your whole goddamn ceremony, the searching doesn't stop. Then you keep startling at every glimpse of someone with a similar back, of someone with the selfsame shoulders. You keep freezing up whenever you hear that selfsame voice.

I keep having more dreams about Jimmy. Like now. I dream that we're standing in the moonlight, on a frozen Canadian lake.

That it's frozen over right up to the U.S. doesn't really surprise us. It's been below zero for weeks. "It's the first time," Jimmy says, "that it's this thick." He plants his heel into it. It doesn't even echo. Black ice.

I want to ask him how he came by those suede gloves. My fingers are tingling; forgot my mittens. When Jimmy lifts his patch, I can see his eye as if the shot were never fired.

I pat my pockets. I dig up a cartridge from the lining, .223-caliber Remington, with a tip capable of producing a gas pressure of around fifty-five thousand psi. Plenty of factual knowledge, and yet I can't begin to explain how we ended up here. I don't feel a gun but I do feel a half-empty pack of cigarettes. I never smoked.

From miles down below our feet lake monsters are circling up. Awakened by Jimmy's treading.

"They're saying that you've let me down," I say, bumping my right hand against my left one until a cigarette comes rolling out of the package. Jimmy gives me a light. Never knew he had a little ring in his eyebrow. Our heads are so near to each other that I can see the closed-up little dent in his skin. We start walking. Breath and smoke trailing. Through a glass landscape.

Jimmy says, "I'm not sure we're going the right way for that clinic."

I reply that he really needs to go, and that I'm absolutely sure it's this way.

Besides me and Jimmy there's no one else on the ice lake, in the night. It starts snowing. I wish he would take my hand, but he doesn't, he hates that. He says we'd better go back. We'll skip the clinic.

I tell him that he has to go there now. Tomorrow will be too late.

"We're not going to stand here arguing, Maria," says Jimmy.

He walks backward over the water and lets the snow come between us. He grins. My God, he's so Chinese. He shouts something that I can't make out but nevertheless understand. Something grand, something generous. But does Jimmy ever mean what he says? I'm too late to nod that I get it, he's already gone. Snowflakes tumble down. Silence.

If what this dream says is true, waking up is the only thing that Jimmy is asking of me.

CHAPTER 18

I park my car past the restaurant. The ice has caused some traffic jams, but I'm still early. This will be a disaster. Even if Victor shows, this will be a disaster. But he won't, I think, know, since he has never kept an appointment before.

I read about a restaurant at the bottom of an iron mine, in Portugal. As I'm walking through the cold, I see us having dinner there: fifteen hundred feet under the ground, left to the mercy of each other and the devastating heat of the earth's core. We're thirsty but the wine is warm. Pearls of sweat gather on our faces but the napkins are all dirty. We're hungry but the meat is tainted. The elevator stays on the surface. We can't think of daylight until we have eaten.

Two nights ago the telephone rang. Martin wasn't home. Nella was asleep. I turned down the volume of the television news. I watched the muted report about a poultry factory farm. A brisk man in coveralls answered questions without making a sound.

The cackling must have been deafening, I saw at least a thousand beaks.

I said my name. Heard right away that it was Victor.

I still hadn't decided if I wanted anything to do with him. When we were still in contact, I wanted to see him as little as possible, and afterward, after Jimmy, I erased every thought of him: exit Victor. I'd been thinking a lot those past days: what if I decide never to speak to Victor again? Then from now on Nella just won't play with Sjanna anymore. Then I just won't invite Mirjam over for coffee anymore. And Jimmy? I haven't thought of him in ten years. How hard can it be to keep that up another forty?

Then Victor called me up. He asked if we could meet somewhere. Dinner, perhaps? Thursday evening?

It took me by surprise. But if he'd called me six months later, it would have been the same.

The news showed footage from the Tour de France, a past edition. A mass sprint just before the finish: pulling and pushing. A rider in a yellow jersey broke away from the rest with force. He was probably the only one showing on the photograph. The anchorman fell silent. Apparently the world had lost another cycling legend.

I said that I would make it, Thursday evening.

Victor answered, "Super."

Super. Apart from the word itself: I tried to make out *how* he said it, whether he meant it. But when you don't trust someone, your perception is distorted. The same for when you trust someone too much.

The next day Martin and I went to our new house. Saying nothing, we painted the hall. Martin started up top, I followed below. I was wearing an old soccer cap. He had a roller, I had a brush.

"It's faster with a roller," he said.

"Not for me."

"It's cleaner with a roller." He looked, swiftly, at my hands. They were covered in paint.

My thoughts dwelled on Victor. The few questions that I wanted to ask him, I kept for myself: I had to know how a gay guy turns straight, how a lazy son of a bitch transforms into a successful businessman, and how a whore becomes a model family man. I had to know whose money he'd used to do that. And what he'd told Mirjam about himself. And why he stayed away from Jimmy's memorial service. And if he was planning to disclose my past to my daughter.

Maybe it was wise to save the first questions for the moment he said yes to the last one.

"What are you going to say to him?" Martin asked.

"I don't know."

"Are you really going to grab a bite together? That sounds positive. You could say that Nella and Sjanna can still play with each other. I would avoid asking tough questions. Ruins the mood. And you won't get an answer anyway."

"Agreed," I said.

But what would it matter if Victor left the table in fury, without answering even one tough question? As long as there was blood, his blood, I would be satisfied.

He would keep his mouth shut to my daughter. After all, he had more to hide than I. For now, he would just have to trust my good manners.

That's what I thought.

* * *

The light in this restaurant is dimmed, the murmurs are muffled, even the cutlery makes hollow sounds against the plates. There's a smell of fresh crustaceans, of roasted game and overpriced fake civility.

He's already there. This time I recognize the back of his head. He's wearing a gray suit. His neck looks even shorter than it did a few days ago. He's sitting by the window. Did he see me cross the parking lot?

I push my hair back and feel the snowflakes under my fingers turn to water. Someone puts away my coat. If Victor saw me, then he knows that I'm inside now. He turns around and looks at me. As I'm walking to him, he gets up. His left hand holds a loose-hanging jacket to his stomach, his right hand reaches out to me. I'd decided at home on giving him another handshake. We sit down.

"Did the snow and ice give you any trouble?" he asks.

Okay, we're talking about the weather. And the weather is bad, very bad. Unusual for the time of the year, all this snow, the cold . . .

"Yes," I say, "it's slippery. Bet you don't get that in Hong Kong."

"It's sixty-five degrees out there right now."

He makes everything sound like a lie, even though I know that you can walk around Kowloon without a coat in January.

Victor talks about his new car. He had a sissy way of talking back then. It hasn't changed a bit, and neither has his taste for designer suits. The rest has ripened, or rotted for ten years, whichever way you want to look at it: Mirjam falls for it and Jimmy couldn't have cared less.

The waiter appears. Have we decided? Victor will have the fish. That would have been my pick. I settle for the duck breast.

I say, "Mirjam is very nice," and gauge his reaction.

"Yes."

"A lovely woman, Victor."

The waiter presents the wine. He uncorks the bottle and invites Victor to sample. Victor smells his glass and nods at the waiter. I say, "A lovely woman, who you don't want to upset with stories about your ex. A man, in your case."

He calmly smears a spoonful of tapenade onto a corner of bread and sticks it in his mouth. He smiles.

"Have you been here before, Maria? Did you know they have a star?"

He puts his knife and fork even straighter next to his plate. Very slowly he entwines his hands into each other and puts some distance between himself and the plate using his knuckles. He lifts up his head and looks at me.

"Your daughter Nella is also very nice. An intelligent little girl that you don't want to hurt by telling her what you dealt in. Weapons and children, in your case."

Before I can answer, our dinner is served. The waiter says something about the meat, the fish. Without listening, we look at each other. Ever since I met Victor again, it feels as if a shard of ice has been placed inside me.

"The point is—" I begin.

"Yes," he says, softly urging, "tell me what the point is! Explain to me why Nella can't play with Sjanna anymore now that you've found out that I'm Sjanna's father. Isn't it lousy enough that you're Nella's mother? That it's your kid who bullied my daughter so ferociously?"

I don't believe for a second that Victor has changed. It's just so astonishing to see what happens when he thinks he cares for someone. Not that I'd prefer to have him conscienceless in front of me, as of old. But this is creepy and I don't know what to do. I shut up.

"Your duck is getting cold," he says.

I fix my gaze on him: "I like to think it's up to me decide what I tell Nella. And the same goes for the moment when I tell her."

He says, "No problem, understood. Completely understood."

We eat in silence. We drink calmly. I think about how I picked him up in that elevator, a long time ago. With his asshole ripped to pieces. How stupid I thought he was. Not pathetic, but stupid. He irritated me. Even when racked with pain, he irritated me. And him? He hated me. Even when I helped him, he hated me. And now it's so damn inconvenient that we hate each other's guts.

The waiter stops by to see if we need anything. He relights the snuffed-out candle. He doesn't think anything of us. Because he's a waiter. We're having dinner like we're well acquainted. We're not. We'll never be. Our kids like to play with each other, and that's why we behave. We eat with knife and fork. Subdued, like everything else in here.

We refuse to grant each other the impression of a pleasant atmosphere. We drink espresso and leave the bonbons untouched.

I think long before asking. And still I do: "Why did you stay away from Jimmy's memorial service?"

He seems surprised. I state date and year. He counts back.

He says, "But then he was with me, in Thailand."

My God, what a lousy excuse. He can't tell the difference between one year and the next. Does this bastard really want me to believe that Jimmy was alive at the time we held that service for him?

"But didn't you get an invitation?" I ask in a raspy voice. "Joe sent you an invitation."

He shakes his head. "I don't know what you're talking about. I really don't. I was working every day, in my bar. Maybe Jimmy caught it in the mail? He took care of the house, carried a gun, he was alive and kicking. We never talked about his illness. Maybe he was saying goodbye or something, I don't know. He stayed for a month. Then he left. Just like that, gone, without a word. I figured he went back to Ontario, or Hong Kong. I didn't go after him. Understood that I wasn't welcome there. His family didn't like me. I never saw him again after that."

I want to get out of here. I don't want to be around Victor any longer. Everything he says is just one big lie, nonsense.

We split the check. Dutch treat; unimaginable when Jimmy was still alive. We put on our coats. I stop him at the revolving door.

"The company," I say, "did he talk to you about that?"

"What do you mean?"

"It didn't have to go bankrupt."

Victor puts on his gloves. "He never gave me a penny. Except for the bar and the Lotus, eventually. I didn't know anything about Jimmy's company. He made me managing director when there wasn't anything left."

"Didn't you find that odd?"

He looks at me.

"What do you mean, odd? Don't you get it? Don't you understand anything? It was Jimmy's way to hold on to me for just a little longer. Before he died he let the company go bust deliberately, because he sure as hell didn't want you in it after his death. Maybe he didn't think you were professional enough or . . ."

He grins.

"Or maybe he thought you didn't deserve it."

I don't want to wake anyone up. Close the front door gently behind me and walk into the dark living room. I fumble for the light switch.

"Jesus, you're late, why didn't you call?"

It sounds more reprimanding than relieved. His hair is flat on one side. I sit next to him on the couch and try to get some volume into it.

"I went out for a drive afterwards," I say. "Did you know that my dad fell asleep on the couch one time when he'd been up waiting for me all night?"

He yawns. "Your cell was off."

I ask, "Anything on the TV? Did she go to bed like a good little girl?"

She's snoring. I get down on my knees to rub the tip of my nose against hers. The noses should barely touch each other. No one else masters this technique. Just the two of us. Maybe one day we'll teach Sjanna and her mother.

Martin lies stretched out over my half. I undress and cuddle up against him. You feel on the inside that it's freezing on the outside.

"So tell me, how did it go?" he mumbles. He turns away from me, dozes off again. I wait until I'm certain that he can't hear me.

"Victor was the last to speak to him," I whisper to the dark.

EPILOGUE

PAST AND PRESENT

It's something I came up with. Something no one has a say in. Especially not Jimmy. The phone can ring. The radio can play. I keep my eyes open the whole time and see everything. Only in my sleep it doesn't work.

I wait until Martin and Nella have gone out. I clear the breakfast table, put the bread back in the freezer, and get the ground meat out for later. Whether I'm folding up laundry or working a hot electric iron, it doesn't matter: whenever I want to, Jimmy and I are walking on the frozen ice lake again. We're no longer looking for a clinic. We don't need to talk about getting better. Jimmy lives. For now.

However: the lake, there's something odd about it. I drop to my knees, wipe away the snow with my sleeve, and try to look through the ice.

I can see air bubbles that didn't reach the surface in time around the wings of a drowned bird. I can't see the water below.

Jimmy says, "When the ice cracks, you need to jump."

"Should I be worried?" I ask.

"Timing is everything, Maria."

He explains how it's possible to jump over a gaping hole with one of those moves you see performed by Kung Fu actors, kicking and tumbling over swaying swords and . . .

Sometimes the phone rings. Or the bell. No problem. Even hours later I can still remember perfectly where I left off.

When Jimmy has nothing left to tell, it stays quiet. Apart from a murmur, monotonous and low.

Jimmy says, "It's not easy being the one who isn't there anymore."

I shrug: "It's not easy being the one who's still here."

"When are you moving, Maria?"

"In three days. So I thought: *Let's get some laundry out of the way.* But I don't like ironing, so I could use a little walk."

He nods contentedly: "Good."

I'm wearing the houndstooth coat, by Givenchy, from one of the boxes. It buttons up easily and doesn't smell like dog food.

"I talked to Victor the other day," I say

"You did leave him in one piece, didn't you?"

"Our daughters are friends."

I don't mention Mirjam. I look aside. It seems as if Jimmy's getting younger: the bags under his eyes have disappeared and his pace grows steadier.

"And how are things with Martin?" he says. "You're together now?"

"Yes," I say, "Nella is our daughter."

"I see, your daughter, yours, a sweet child . . ."

He smiles, as if he sees her every day.

"Where are we?" I ask, concerned because I don't see his parents' house, no boat, no landing, shore nowhere in sight.

Jimmy doesn't stop. He doesn't answer. He doesn't even wait for me. Suddenly he gets on my nerves, he's just as goddamn selfish as ever! I catch up with him, panting.

"Victor insinuated that you let the company go to pot deliberately when you got ill. That you were looking for an excuse to fire me, so that I couldn't succeed you. Why was that? Were you jealous? Afraid that I would do better than you? Why the hell did you disappear all of a sudden without saying anything?"

"Disappear?" he shouts, seemingly insulted. "Dear girl, what are you talking about? I'm standing *here*, right in front of you!"

I ask again why the company had to go bankrupt. I slip, I'm the one who falls, backward on the hard, cold surface. The murmur is coming from underneath the ice.

When I'm back on my feet, I notice that I'm the only one who's out of breath. Jimmy laughs and tells me not to get all worked up.

He asks, "How old is she now, Nella?"

"Ten."

"You've wanted kids all your life, Maria."

I think: *That's not true. No, that's not true.* Or is it? I should ask Martin. Maybe I wanted kids before I went to work for Jimmy? After that, I never thought of it again. Except when Jimmy brought it up. Or when they happened to cross my path. Mr. and Mrs. Yang's baby in Beijing, the children that Jimmy found shot in Chechnya, Noah in Karachi, and in Quetta, Reza and Najim. Who wants to start thinking about kids of her own after that? I just want to continue working, until I die, until everyone dies, I was good at what I did, damn good.

I put away the ironed clothes. Then I gather empty lemonade bottles and take the shopping bag off the hook in the wardrobe. I put them in it. Ten empty bottles. I want Jimmy to stop walking around on the frozen water. I want him to stop me.

He does. His face is dead serious, just like on the day he made me fire my first Kalashnikov, out in the desert. He says softly, "Of course you would have carried on our business. Better than me."

He grabs my collar and says urgingly, "You never would have quit. Do you hear me, Maria? Never! Never!"

Sometimes I apply little variations. It all depends on what I'm in the mood for. Usually it's sunny, sometimes it gets dark above the lake. The words always stay the same. And the ice is always there. And everything always ends in the same way: the icy floor under our feet is raised. Not to staggering heights, and nothing snaps, but we turn away from each other with lightning speed and run to different sides.

I stop and see Jimmy standing fifty feet away from me. I look at him, speechless. I can't believe what he just admitted.

The ice splits and cracks. Water spills over the edges, not much, looks like ink. The lake breaks, it splashes, we drift away from each other. I want to go to him, to hit him, but I can't get too close to the edge of my floe.

I put a hand in the pocket of the coat that I swore never to wear again after Jimmy's party. I discover something flat, something small, a jade rooster, Jimmy's talisman, he never got it.

I see how Jimmy puts his hands to his mouth. I look intently at his face. There's a lot of noise around us, of seething water and ice breaking up. Jesus, he's drifting so incredibly far away. He shouts. Gestures that I'm forgetting something. That I should do something. But what? Suddenly I get it, hear it!

"Jump!" he screams. "Jump, Maria, for God's sake: jump!"

The water's rising up to my ankles. I look at Jimmy. I nod. Then I turn my back on him. I clasp my fingers around the talisman and squeeze, hard.

I count to three. At one, I bend my knees. At two, I squat down. I make myself flatter than a frog. Three. I jump.

ACKNOWLEDGMENTS

Various chapters from this book have been published as stories in *Hollands Maandblad*, with thanks to Bastiaan Bommeljé for his most thorough and instructive comments. My sincerest gratitude goes to my Magnificent Seven: Harry Vaandrager, Pim Verhulst, Paul Sebes, Willem Bisseling, Charlie Olsen, Philip Marino, and Peter Miller. They carefully constructed a bridge across the Atlantic with a most startling view from the other side.

ML   11-12